An Untitled Love

Olivia Gaines

OLIVIA GAINES

Davonshire House Publishing
PO Box 9716
Augusta, GA 30916

© 2015 Olivia Gaines, Cheryl Aaron Corbin
Copy Editor: Gayla Leath
Cover: koou-graphics
Olivia Gaines Make Up and Photograph by Latasla Gardner Photography

ASIN: B019J7M8T0
ISBN-13: 978-0692605356
ISBN-10: 0692605355

1 2 3 4 5 6 7 10 9 8

First Davonshire House Publishing December 2015

DEDICATION

For Chip. Thank you for giving me the kind of love that has no title.

"Easy reading is damn hard writing."
-   Nathaniel Hawthorne

ACKNOWLEDGMENTS

To all the fans, friends and supporters of the dream as well
as the Facebook community of writers who keep me
focused, inspired and moving forward.

Write On!

Augusta Writers

Also by Olivia Gaines

The Slice of Life Series

- The Perfect Man
- Friends with Benefits
- A Letter to My Mother
- The Basement of Mr. McGee
- A New Mommy for Christmas

The Slivers of Love Series

- The Cost to Play
- Thursday in Savannah
- Girl's Weekend
- Beneath the Well of Dawn
- Santa's Big Helper

The Davonshire Series

- Courting Guinevere
- Loving Words
- Vanity's Pleasure

The Blakemore Files

- Being Mrs. Blakemore
- Shopping with Mrs. Blakemore
- Dancing with Mr. Blakemore
- Cruising with the Blakemores
- Dinner with the Blakemores
- Loving the Czar

The Value of a Man Series

- My Mail Order Wife
- A Weekend with the Cromwell's

Other Novellas

- North to Alaska

- The Brute & The Blogger

- A Better Night in Vegas

Other Novels

- A Menu for Loving
- Turning the Page

Chapter 1- Boarding the Train

It may have been the craziest idea Orlando Flynn had ever come up with in his life, but it was all he had to work with, so he was going for broke. In the end, he surmised his financials could end up in the same state, yet this had to work. The nearly four hour drive to Kennesaw, Georgia gave him enough time to smooth out his offer and make her believe that his plan was feasible. It was crazy, but again it was the only ace up his sleeve and he was going to play the card he had been holding. All he had to do was ask the question. The worst she could say is no. If she did say no, she owed him her life and he was going to call in his marker.

He needed this.

He needed her to get on board and go along.

The drive up I-75 was pleasant enough for a Friday morning as he listened to classical music to keep his head clear. Self-doubt and reason had left him two days ago when he got the phone call which made him sleep for two nights curled up in a ball in his bed. The sheer amazement of the level of 'shitty' that people could be to each other soured his stomach. The nausea was overtaking him as he pulled into a rest stop making a beeline for the bathroom. A greasy egg and bacon sandwich, orange juice and coffee coagulated in his stomach and came up though his esophagus much rougher than it had gone down. The lack of sleep, along with the inability to keep anything in his stomach was becoming more than he could handle. The auto flush on the toilet signaled that it was time for him to get up off his knees and get back on the road.

Orlando drove slowly as he made the exit off I-75 to the

I-575 exchange, making his way up the road to Kennesaw. *I hope she will be happy to see me.* He hadn't physically seen Jacquetta Mason in almost a year. Twice a month, like clockwork, they spoke on the phone; she sharing pieces of her life and him doing the same. She was probably the only woman, outside of his mother, who truly knew and understood him. That's why, when he came up with his crazy idea, he knew it would be a starting point to gaining her compliance.

He exited the freeway to Douglas Street, making a left on Monroe, a right on Jackson, one more left, if he remembered it correctly, to Baker Avenue to her apartment building. It wasn't the best neighborhood in Kennesaw, but it was livable. The flowers he held in his hand were droopy because, like an idiot, he purchased them at a little shop outside of his hometown of Venture, Georgia instead of purchasing them fresh in Kennesaw. He had a one-track mind, and to keep the train from derailing he had to keep the engine in gear and his foot on the pedal pushing all of it forward.

In the rearview mirror he checked his teeth. His breath was still tart from the pit stop. He frowned at the stench when he blew into his hand and inhaled sour. Orlando rummaged through the truck's arm rest finding a piece of peppermint. The question surged through his head but he refused to think about when and where he had acquired said candy. It was gummy and gooey. It reminded him of the candy at the bottom of his mother's purse. *I have no idea where this came from but my breath needs it.*

Entering the building, another stench drifted up his nose as the smell of unwashed bodies saturated the elevator he was forced to ride in to get up to the 8th floor where she lived. Nervous knees knocked together as he stood outside her door, his fist suspended in midair wanting to knock but afraid of his own screwed up logic that had gotten him this far.

Knock fool.

Lean forward, let your knuckles make contact with the wood and knock.

Two minutes later he was still standing there when the lady across the hall, who had been watching him through her peephole, yelled what he was also thinking. "You need to go ahead and knock fool! Why you standing there like an idiot with those droopy ass flowers. You came this far— knock already," she yelled.

Based on his conversations with Jacquetta, he knew who she was. Orlando half turned to take a look at the nosey cheerleader's door.

"Thank you Ms. Bonner," he told the nosey neighbor.

"How the hell you know my name?"

On the other side of the door, his voice was also heard as a surprised Jacquetta opened her front door to find Orlando Flynn on her doorstep.

With flowers.

Arguing with her nosey old neighbor.

He was failing miserably at feebly trying to prove he wasn't an agent of the government sent to spy on her.

"Orlando..." Jacquetta said softly, "What are you doing here?"

"You know this man 'Quetta? He ain't a government agent sent here to spy on us about not having Obamacare?" Ms. Bonner wanted to know.

"No Ms. Bonner, he is my friend," she told the floor watch dog.

She grabbed him by the arm and pulled him inside the door, closing and locking it behind her. At the same time her phone rang. Jacquetta held up a finger, asking him to hold fast as she answered the phone. It was of course Ms. Bonner.

"No ma'am, I am fine. He is a dear friend," she said waiting, trying to get a word in edgewise. "No, I don't know why he was standing there for two minutes waiting to knock... yes, he should have called first...yes, you are right, men have changed. Oh you did...he has a suitcase in his truck... I didn't know he was planning to stay the night. I know, yes, you are right, it is the oldest trick in the book," she said as she took the sad, limp flowers from his hand. "Yes ma'am, I am putting them in water now," she told the old lady.

After a few more yes ma'ams and no ma'ams, Jacquetta hung up the phone to stare at him with more than a mild curiosity. "I can't wait to hear what crazy ass idea you concocted in that head of yours that made you get up at six in the morning to start driving to Kennesaw," she said as she looked at her watch. It was a few minutes after 10 am.

"Can I at least get a hug and an *I'm so glad to see you Orlando!*" He said as he held out his arms.

She stepped into the mass of body that was her friend and got enveloped in a warm embrace. She rose onto her tiptoes to plant a kiss on his jaw as she patted him on the back. Pulling away she told him, "I just put on some coffee, come and let me pour you a cup while I listen to this crazy idea of yours." She made her way to the kitchen and poured a hot steamy cup of Joe for him, and gave it to him black and sweet, just the way he liked it. A half a cup was poured for herself, since she'd already had two this morning.

"How do you know it is a crazy idea?"

"You drove for four hours with a bunch of half dead flowers," she said flatly. "What, no box of chocolates or a diamond ring?"

The expression on his face made her stop in her tracks. "I can't wait to hear this...hold up, let me sit down so when I pass out, I don't hit my head," Jacquetta told him.

He watched her small frame take a seat on the couch, one leg tucked neatly under her as she held her coffee mug with both hands. The smile that lit up her face was part of the reason why he was here. Jacquetta was genuinely a good person with a kind heart. She was also a loving woman who took care of those around her, making everyone she came into contact with feel included. Her emotions were also genuine which showed through her art. The woman was a helluva artist.

"Can't I come check on my friend?" he asked coyly.

"Nope. You want something big. You may as well spit it out so I can tell you no, feed you lunch and send you back home," she said to him. Her eyes were watching him over the rim of the mug.

"Not gonna happen, my friend. You owe me a huge favor and I have shown up in person to collect on that debt," he said.

Jacquetta sat the coffee cup down and leaned back into the couch, her chin resting upon her knuckles, while one hand was on her hip.

"This better not be some delayed booty call Orlando...cause that shit ain't gonna fly," she told him.

"No...," he said, thinking hard. "You think I would drive for four hours, all the way up here to ask you to have sex with me? That is the most ridiculous thing I have ever heard!"

"Then why are you here?" she wanted to know.

"Oh, I came to take you to get a blood test," he said with a sheepish grin.

"What, do you need half of my liver or some bone marrow

or something?" She frowned as she leaned forward, listening to him with her full attention. Her face registering the level of disbelief she knew was going to accompany whatever request he had in that head of his.

"No, I am healthy as a horse," he said as he winked at her with the sly innuendo that he was hung like one as well. His smile seemed to brighten as he looked at her once more with a twinkle in his eye, delivering the words that physically knocked her over, "No, I came to marry you!"

Chapter 2- That's Just Unheard of

The silence between them was so loud, Orlando swore he heard a rat urinating on a cotton ball. She said nothing after she fell over on her side on the couch, immobile, for five minutes total. He knew this because he set the timer on his watch as he monitored her reaction. She was looking at him like he had lost his damned mind. A muscle in her right jaw twitched at the three minute mark, but other than that, Jacquetta had not moved.

Nor had she blinked.

When the six minute mark approached, he held up his hand. "Let me explain. I was thinking I could stay until Sunday as we worked out the details of getting you moved to Venture. We can go get the blood test done today and when I come back on Friday with the rental truck to move you, we can get married before we hit the road."

Jacquetta still had not blinked.

"I mean, when I spoke with you two weeks ago, you said you weren't seeing anyone, right?" he asked.

Finally, arguments were starting to fill the void in her head where his words had sucked out the reasoning with his request. "Yeah and two weeks ago you were engaged to be married to Becca."

"Becca is now pregnant by some French dude named Beauvais, or some shit, and she is coming home in two weeks," he said.

"And marrying me is going to do what, help you save face?"

He threw up his hands. "See I knew you would understand!"

She was shaking her head. "No, I don't understand. I don't understand at all how taking home a black woman to your highly conservative family and town is going to help you save face."

"If I walk in with you as my wife, no one, I mean no one will ask me questions about Becca, that French asshole, or feel sorry for me that I got dumped via text message," he said.

For a minute Jacquetta saw the pain in his eyes and the vulnerability. She asked, "And if I marry you to save face, what happens in a year when you are healed? What do we do then?"

The look on his face was priceless as he said with pride, "In a year you will be painting rabbits on the wall of the nursery for the arrival of our first child!"

This was the point when Jacquetta became lightheaded and a grabbed a pillow on the couch to tether her back to this world. The world Orlando was residing in did not seem to be based in any form of reality. "I don't believe you Orlando. I can't even sit upright now I am so bowled over by all of this," she said as she lay the back of her hand across her eyes.

Orlando moved over to the couch, taking her hand in his. "'Quetta, we love each other... right?"

She partially sat up on the couch. "It's not the same kind of love. I am not certain it is the kind of love I would have even agreed to be tested to give you a piece of my liver. The kind of love we have it...it...it's just not the same."

"Which is what makes it perfect. We both have had the kind of love where we gave everything and we both have been crushed by selfish people who have used us...I mean honestly. I paid for that woman to travel a bit before the wedding... and she goes and gets knocked up on my dime! Now she is coming home to rub it in my face... I am not going out like that!" He said adamantly. The fire and passion in his eyes was unmistakable.

"So you want to rub it in her face that you are coming home with something exotic as well?"

"You and I know each other. We have the kind of love that, you know, I will walk through a maelstrom of bullets to protect you...there is nothing I wouldn't do for you," he said to her.

She was looking at him. "... And I took on a swarm of Afghan rebels to save you, but that is not enough to build a marriage on with you Orlando," she told him.

"It is more than enough for me, because if there is one woman I trust in the world more than my own Mama, it is you. I will never wake up a day in my life wondering if my wife loves me for me," he said, his mouth getting dry. "You have seen me at my best. You have seen me at my worst and you still love me," he said.

"But I have not seen you in the role as my man. My rescuer, my friend, yes, but as the father of my children... Orlando, I can't see it," she told him.

"You have seen me naked on more than one occasion...," he started to say.

"Yes, but I was pulling shrapnel out of your ass cheeks, so I was not looking at the goods like, 'Oh yeah, I want some of that'," she said.

Suddenly he stood. He kicked off his shoes, pulled his shirt over his head and was reaching for his belt buckle. Jacquetta jumped up off the couch. "Wait, hold up Orlando, what do you think you are doing?"

He didn't stop, but yanked the belt open, and pulled down his pants, underwear included. He stepped out of his jeans and stood before her wearing nothing but his socks. Jacquetta started looking around the room like three angry bees had just flew into the window fighting like ninjas. Orlando, obviously unfazed, grabbed her coffee mug, went to the kitchen and started refreshing her coffee.

Stuttering a bit as she spoke, not believing what she was actually seeing, "...uh...ah...well...Orlando, I mean why...uhmm... are walking around my apartment wearing only a pair of socks?"

"Because this is how I walk around in my own house. I also wanted you to have a chance to check out the goods so you will know what you will be working with for the rest of your life," he told her as he stood before her with a fresh cup of coffee.

"This is insane! And put your damned clothes back on!" she yelled at him.

She squinted her eyes as she cocked her head. "Is this some sort of delayed PTSD or a mental breakdown?"

"No...you said you could not see me as your man. I stand before you bare, heart in hand, asking you to share a life with me. I want you to know that all of this sexy..." he said as he wiggled his dangling parts. "... Is all yours from this day forth."

"Oh, lucky me," she told him. "You know I am not going to agree to this Orlando."

"You are going to agree to it and here is why," he told her with no emotion in his voice. There were several relevant points he made starting with her having no personal form of transportation. Secondly, he told her it made no sense to pay rent on an apartment and a studio space for her art. Third, he explained that her art was all over Atlanta on commission and without a car, she didn't know if the pieces had sold or not because she had no way to physically check.

"I will go home and build you a dedicated shed in the back yard as your own personal studio with fantastic morning light. I will get you an SUV, not new, but in very good condition so on the weekends you can haul your stuff to shows to sell. Last but not least, if sales are steady, in a year's time, you will have your own gallery after the birth of our first child. What is mine is yours and what is yours is mine," he told her.

Jacquetta was still shaking her head no. "I guess with this child that I am giving you that I will be expected to share your bed to create it?"

"Yes we will share a bed starting tonight. We will get to that other part when you are ready," he told her.

"But what if I don't feel that way about you?" she asked him.

"Eventually, you will get thirsty enough…and you will need a drink," he said as he gazed deep into her eyes. "I plan to be your bottle of water."

"Do you feel that way about me…I mean, I don't want to be in bed with a man who has to imagine I am someone else in order for us to procreate," she told him.

"When I make love to you, there will never be any doubt in my mind who I am in bed with," he was still gazing into her eyes when he spoke to her.

To her amazement, her heart fluttered a bit.

"I'll be good to you. I will treat you with love and respect, and if you give that back to me, we will be fine," he told her.

"What if in two years you want to be free?'

"I only plan to marry once. I have decided that it is you I am going to marry, so it doesn't matter five, ten, or twenty years from now, you will still be my wife."

"My answer is no," she told him.

He said nothing as he reached for his pants on the floor, grabbed his wallet and pulled out a piece of weathered paper that he had laminated, handing it to her.

"You can't say no. I am calling in my marker," he said

flatly.

Orlando Flynn was right. She owed him her life. Almost six years ago she had written him the note with the promise that she would honor it. It never occurred to her that he would call in the marker, especially not this way.

Chapter 3 – The Unsung Hero

Kandahar, Afghanistan, 2010

The vehicle rolled down the sandblasted road hitting bumps, ruts and every pothole in the desert hellhole. Sergeant First Class Jacquetta Mason sat in the back of the military truck behind the mass of medical supplies being shipped to the city. The art work she was sent in to evaluate was hidden inside the containers. Thus far the runs in and out of the city had been very successful, but more importantly, uneventful. She believed today would be no different until the vehicle started to slow.

"Everything okay up there?" She called out to Callahan, the driver.

Callahan yelled back, "It's some kind of blockage in the road."

"Can you get around it?"

"Don't look like it Sarge," Callahan yelled.

"Drive right through it," she commanded.

"Can't barbed wire and...."

He didn't finish his sentence. Bullets whizzed by her head as the sound of the metal rounds tore through the soft sides of the truck. She could hear Callahan groaning as he yelled out, "Sarge I'm hit. I'm hit!"

"Stay calm Callahan, I'm making my way," she told him. She checked the clip in her weapon to make sure it was fully loaded as she used the slot in the side of the vehicle to brace her weapon and began to return fire. "Put as much pressure on it as you can, Callahan, I am making my way to you," she yelled as she fired off a few more rounds.

The direction of the gunfire was becoming too intense and unless she wanted to become a chunk of Swiss cheese, she stopped shooting and got down low. On her belly she lay in the rear of the truck and waited. The firestorm ended as voices could be heard surrounding the vehicle. Jacquetta slid under the tarp. The voices were becoming louder as scurrying feet climbed into the truck and started to unload the cargo.

Still your breathing.

Box after box left the truck and the bright light of the sun was illuminating not only the back of the truck but her hiding place. A yell was heard, she understood the word '*woman*' in Arabic and a hand was on her ankle. Jacquetta kicked and fought, bringing her 9mm upward and firing three shots, taking out a few of the men who were dragging her out of the truck. There was nowhere for her to run as she came face to face with the Taliban soldiers who stood at the back of the truck.

"Don't kill her! Lacoste needs fresh women, we can sell her," the leader of the group called out. A black sack was thrown over her head as her body was yanked and tugged. Jacquetta could feel hands on her head, pushing it downward as she was shoved into the back of a vehicle with her feet and hands bound. She wiggled against the binding that held her hands trying to fight, trying to free her hands and feet but it was of no use. A fist made contact with her stomach. Her breathing was becoming short. She began to hyperventilate until she felt water being thrown over her face through the black cloth sack that shrouded her head.

Am I about to be water boarded?

Stay calm.

Her body was dumped on the floor of a vehicle. The drive seemed to be well over an hour. Once they arrived at the their destination, Jacquetta was pulled from the back of the vehicle and flung across an animal she assumed to be a camel. It smelled horrible. Even worse, her bladder was full and in a few minutes she wasn't going to have no choice but to let it go.

A saving grace was the bag over her head, it reduced a great deal of the dust which seemed to almost strangle her as they rode. They came to a stop as she was pulled, not so gently, from the animal to land in a thud on the ground. A woman in a *ḥijāb* pulled the bag off her head. Jacquetta studied her surroundings trying desperately to adjust her eyes to the bright sunlight. She was in the middle of nowhere.

No trees.

No landmarks.

Just sand.

Sand.

More sand.

The woman untied her hands and feet. "Pee-pee, go," she told Jacquetta.

She looked around. *Great, I'm stuck in a really big litter box.* She unfastened her uniform pants, spread her legs and squatted. The relief was so wonderful, she thought she was hearing things.

In the middle of nowhere, a helicopter was landing. The woman in the black covering snapped at her, "Come. We go."

Struggling to get her pants up, Jacquetta was shoved into the helicopter and it lifted into the air. Desperation consumed her as the comprehension that she would never be found became a reality. Out of fear for her immortal soul, suicide was not an option to her.

I only have to survive.

Survive and find a way home.

In three days, she had been transferred four times. Several instances she had been examined in the most humiliating manner, with fingers probing none to gently, her blood was drawn without her consent, and she witnessed one of the men mixing a powder into the water he tried to give her. She knocked the cup out of his hand, spilling the contents. This resulted in a blow to her mid-section that caused her bladder to let loose. She understood what he spat at her...she was to be sold to the highest bidder.

"You won't be so high and mighty when those men finish with you...you will wish you had submitted to me!" her smelly, hairy, big bellied captor said with a thick accent.

She spoke back to him, knowing he understood English. Jacquetta told her captor, "I would rather submit to a camel before I allow you to touch me."

He hit her again, this time in her back, right above her kidneys, buckling her to her knees again.

"We shall see about that," he told her. He made a series of yells calling forth six men who lifted her from the floor, carrying her outside the small building where she was being held to be loaded into a black SUV with darkly tinted windows. They drove through the night until they reached the outskirts of Abu Dhabi where she was transferred to another vehicle and driven into the bowels of the city.

Somewhere deep inside Abu Dhabi, in a series of rooms, she was placed in a shower, her skin scrubbed with a roughly made soap and her body adorned in the finest silk clothes before being dragged into a dimly lit room. When she was redressed, she had not been given any underwear to put on and the silk was see through. She tried to avoid standing in front of any direct lighting in the semi-dark room, although the men who brought her in, intentionally placed her in front of the light. Smoke filled the sour air as men in keffiyehs talked, joked and fondled the women brought into the room for auction. In the center of the dank space, four feet from the auction stage, a high stakes card game was being played. Jacquetta understood that she was the prize thrown in to sweeten the pot.

"If you like a fiery woman to warm your bed…this one is just the thing. Her value isn't as high as the blond or the redhead, but this one is trainable," the large bearded man told the group of men at the table.

Jacquetta was hauled to the table by the dog collar around her neck for a closer view. One man attempted to touch her breasts to make certain they were real, and she slapped his hand. This brought a rousing chorus of laughs and bawdy comments.

"I wonder if she would slap my ass like that as well," another man with an oddly trimmed mustache bellowed.

"As ugly as you are Lacoste, she would slap your face and probably confuse that with your ass," chuckled the bearded man.

Six men sat at the table. One was a white American who only gave her a mild glance as if he had no interest in her. The white man spoke in Arabic to the game players, "Are we in a comedy club or are we playing cards?"

"I will play for my own freedom," she said.

One of the men slapped her, knocking her off her feet. The American didn't move or turn his head to look at her. The Arab, in the white keffiyeh, pulled a large knife on the man who had struck her.

"The value is reduced if the product is damaged," the leader said. "You owe me ten thousand for marking her face."

One of the men pushed at the American to help her up. The American whispered as he helped her to her feet, "How much is your freedom worth?"

"I have fifty thousand reasons for you to get me out of

here," she whispered.

"Okay," he said to her. "I will take that as a verbal marker," he said in an even lower voice.

She didn't quite know what happened next, but in seconds the six men were on the ground and she was being lugged outside by the American and shoved into another dark SUV. Although no one was chasing them, her rescuer drove like a bat out of hell to an airstrip where an unmarked plane sat on a makeshift tarmac. He moved quickly, grabbing her by the arm, almost hefting her off her feet and tossing her inside the back of the plane. Her rescuer immediately locked the door and yelled to the pilot, "Go! Go! Take off!" The plane began to taxi down the airstrip rising above the oasis of a city in the middle of the desert.

Jacquetta was shaking but trying desperately to stay calm. "Can I get a piece of paper?" she asked her rescuer in a shaky voice. Her hand was trembling as she wrote on the linen sheet.

Feeble attempts were made to cover her thighs and legs with the silky material she wore. Nothing much was left to the imagination in the outfit.

"A life for a life. "Jacquetta Mason

She signed her name and introduced herself, "Thank you, I am Jacquetta Mason," she told the man.

"I know who you are. I was sent to retrieve you. Orlando Flynn, Army Special Forces," he told her. Jacquetta handed him the paper.

"Here is my marker. I owe you my life," she told him. Her hand was still quivering as he accepted the note.

"I may call you on this," Orlando told her as he placed the paper in his wallet.

"I will honor it," she replied as tears began to run down her face.

Five days.

Five days and she was nearly forced into the sex slave trade by a winning hand in a card game. The ugly truth also dawned on her, what if Orlando hadn't been there to be the one who saved her, but instead he had been one of the men who was there to play the game and win the prize. Stupidly she had offered money to a stranger who could have made her predicament worse. The overwhelming feeling of helplessness overcame her and salty droplets of tears poured so deeply from her, she felt as if her soul was being emptied. Orlando Flynn moved closer pulling her onto his lap, wrapping a soft blanket over her legs covering as much of her body that the material failed to shield.

"You are safe, you can sleep now," he told her.

She allowed his words to comfort her as she leaned into his chest, curled into a ball, trying desperately to get warm. The scent of bergamot wafted into her nose as the warmth from his skin seeped into her. For nearly five days she had been awake, trying to remember sounds, smells, potential locations of where her captors were taking her. *Stay awake so you can fight.* She had eaten very little. She had slept even less and she was nearly dehydrated. Jacquetta knew she would not have been able to hold out one more day.

A silent prayer was said thanking the Heavens that Orlando Flynn was one of the good guys. The marker she gave him she would honor if he ever needed her to do anything for him. He had but to ask.

She never expected that almost six years later he would show up to claim the kitty, in the figurative and literal sense of the word.

Chapter 4- Understanding

Kennesaw, Georgia, 2015

Jacquetta looked at the laminated piece of paper she had written nearly six years ago when Orlando had rescued her. She made a promise that when he came to claim his winnings, she would honor her word. He was here and her word was starting to choke the hell out of her.

"I believe the marker was for $50,000," she told him.

"I don't want money. Besides, the marker says *a life for a life*. I saved yours and you owe me," he told her.

"Yeah, but..." she started to say.

"There are no buts in your response. I saved your life and you made me a promise that you would honor this. I expect you to be a woman of your word. I need you. I need you to honor this," he told her. The laminated paper he shoved at her.

Her head pressed into the pillow on the couch. She rubbed her eyes as she looked over at him, still only wearing socks, staring at her. "Could you please put something on?" she asked him.

"Why? Is all of this sexiness getting to you?" he asked, with one eyebrow arched.

"No, you need to sit down and I don't want your naked ass on my couch," she told him.

He looked around the apartment. It was sparse. Only one of her paintings hung on the wall. "You don't have much to move do you?"

"All of my stuff is in storage. I saw no need to haul it up here, it is not the best neighborhood," she said softly.

"I have the basics in my house. It is four bedrooms, with

an eat-in kitchen, a formal dining room, living room and a den. I have a bedroom set, a table in the kitchen, a couch and my Big Daddy chair in the den but the other rooms are empty," he told her.

"This is the house you bought last year, right...the fixer-upper craftsman?"

"Yeah, it is a nice house. I figured with some of your paintings, a few pics of us around the place, some drapes, and your artistic touch, it will look really nice and homey," he said as he pulled his underwear on and took a seat. "It also has a big front porch, which will look great with a couple of rockers, some planter boxes with flowering colorful plants."

She watched him with a new appreciation...*husband. Father. Potential lover...*

"Out of curiosity, how do you plan to spring this on your very white parents and family?"

"When I head back, I will get my brothers to help me get your studio set up in the backyard. That's when I will tell them. As for the rest, we will reveal our union at the annual Fourth of July family cookout," he told her.

She knew the event. He had spoken of it often over the years. It was started by his father, who had owned the local hardware store. A hardware store Orlando now owned. Each year he would roll out the giant grill as families would come and throw grillables on the flame and sit in the park all day on the Fourth. Orlando explained that it had grown over the years with portable water slides added along with games and tournaments with prizes. The whole town would be there for the annual event and the fireworks display once the sun set. Jacquetta could almost envision the scene that she could capture on film, then paint the slice of Americana.

"And what am I supposed to do with myself in Venture,

Georgia?"

"Whaddaya mean? You will be my wife. You will paint, join the women's league, sign up to work on a charity and take care of me and our kids," he said with surprise in his voice.

"Take care of you?"

"Yes. Take care of me and I will take care of you. My Mama never worked outside the home. Well, during the holidays and planting seasons, she lends a hand at the store...you can do the same if you want," he said.

"So you expect me to give up my life to move to the bottom of Georgia to be June Cleaver?"

"No, I expect you to give up whatever you call yourself trying to accomplish here, with no success, to come share my life as we build something together as Jacquetta Flynn, wife, mother, artist," he told her. "Jacquetta, you understand what you and I have. We love each other, but we also like each other. I like spending time with you. I enjoy your company and you enjoy mine." he asserted.

She couldn't argue with that portion of his logic.

He moved in close. "Quetta, you will never have to worry again about paying rent, a car note, or stocking the fridge. I'm not rich, but the store does well, and we will be okay. I bought the house from a foreclosure at the bank. I did the repairs myself and it is paid for...our home is paid for – there is no mortgage," he said.

Jacquetta half leaned upwards on her elbow. "You didn't expect me to say yes, because you don't even have a ring," she said as she exhaled.

Orlando reached for his pants on the floor. His fingers dug around the jeans pocket and brought out a small box. On one knee he knelt before her as his brown eyes stared into hers, "Jacquetta Lynette Mason, will you do me the honor of being my wife?"

It was so sincere and the ring was so pretty that she found herself grinning and saying, "Yes, I will."

Well, that wasn't much of a fight.

He jumped to his feet clapping his hands together after slipping the princess cut diamond onto her finger. "Great! I am starving, let's get the blood test done, grab something to eat and take a look at the storage unit, so I can know what size truck to rent," he told her.

"I have a lot to close out in a week," she said absently as she eyed the ring. It wasn't too big. The diamond wasn't too small. The detail work on the setting was damned near artistic as she eyed the craftsmanship. It was a very nice ring.

I love it.

Orlando was putting his pants on. "And I hate needles. Can we do the blood test first?" he wanted to know.

"Sure, Orlando." She watched him get dressed as she took a good look at him.

Husband.

Father.

Lover...

What am I getting myself into?

We have so much history together in a relationship that was always untitled.

Now, he is to be my husband.

The father of my children.

My lover.

"You okay Jacquetta?" he asked with that same boyish charm that earned him free drinks, free lap dances and unbridled trust from every woman he came in contact with.

Orlando had proven himself trustworthy on many occasions outside of the one in that seedy dark room in Abu

Dhabi. There were so many memories between them from the time of her rescue until now. From Abu Dhabi they traveled back to the war zone to connect with his unit. There were a few scrapes they had gotten themselves into trying to get out of Afghanistan and back to Iraq where she had to still fight and save him as well. His team had come under fire and a dirty bomb exploded, sending shrapnel in every direction. Orlando shielded her with his body, earning a butt full of metal shards. The metal pieces she picked out with care using tweezers and a boatload of patience. Both understood that getting her back to safety wasn't as easy as she had hoped, but somehow, together they made it.

Even after she returned to her duty station in Italy, he would visit every six months to check on her. Once she completed her contracted tour of duty with NATO, Jacquetta got out of the Army, relocated from Italy and studied art in Paris for a year. Orlando even came to France twice that year to visit her there as well; to make sure she was okay. They talked every two weeks and knew the minutest details of each other's lives.

Irony.

I am already sharing a life with him.

"Just wrapping my head around being off the market," she told him.

"Don't worry, I'm all the man you will ever need," he said and winked at her.

"I have no doubts you are going to keep me busy," she said as she found her shoes and door keys. "Let's go and get that bloodtest."

Chapter 5- You're Safe Now

After the blood test, the weekend sped by. To her utter amazement, her big strong fiancé acted like a four-year-old when he saw the needle. Jacquetta had to hold his hand to keep him still for the blood draw.

All during lunch, Orlando continuously checked the puncture site on his arm for damage and signs of infection. Jacquetta was over the ridiculous behavior. She thought of a time when he was in control and felt powerful by asking, "Do you remember that evening in Pisa when those three Asian men kept hitting on me? They were martial arts experts and you took them on...taking them out one at time."

His eyes left the spot where the tape was around his arm. "Yeah, those guys were jerks," he told her, his face stern with anger from the memory she invoked.

"Do you know what you want to eat?" she asked and just like that, the bandage and blood draw was all but forgotten. He ordered a large helping of protein, way too many carbs and washed it down with a sugary sweet soda. The food arrived and his focus went right to the large slab of meat he ordered.

It was a pleasant meal as he told her all about the town of Venture, Flynn Hardware and the natural sunlight in the backyard. "I know the perfect spot to put your new studio," he told her with a smile so bright she was drawn in.

"I was thinking that I may want to paint some images and scenes on the walls of the house," she mentioned out of curiosity.

"Like Frescos or something?" he asked as he sucked the meat off the rib bone.

"Or something...," she responded.

"Sure. It is our home, make it as welcoming as you want,"

he told her. He continued to eat as if his request to her was as natural as the day was long in summer. It was almost as if a relief had washed over him and now he could breathe.

"Orlando you seem so sure about this," she said.

He stopped masticating the half cow he ordered for lunch. "I know you. I feel lucky to have you in my life. I feel even luckier to have you consent to be my wife," he said to her. "I mean, I am kind of nervous, but not for the reason you think."

"So tonight…were you planning to…you know try to…?" she asked shyly.

"What are you asking? If I am planning to make love to you tonight?"

"Yeah, I mean…we are engaged and all," she said to him.

To her surprise he said quickly, "No. You are not ready for that yet. How about we take our time, get used to living together… sharing space."

"When I get to Venture will I be expected to sleep in the same bed with you as well?"

He surprised her again when he told her, "You asked that once. My answer is still the same. Yes. You will. We will practice sharing the bed this weekend so it won't be weird come Friday."

Her face was deadpan, when she told him, "Heaven forbid it get weird."

He waggled his brows and winked at her again.

Orlando Flynn was a walking conundrum. As large and as fit as he was, he was squeamish about the oddest things. Some she knew, others she would learn in the weeks to come. The first thing she learned was, even though he liked to be undressed, he didn't sleep in the nude. The second thing she learned, the man was a very light sleeper.

Orlando also learned something very important about

her he didn't know; Jacquetta suffered from night terrors. Friday night was uncomfortable for them both in several ways. For him, he had never shared a bed with her and sleeping so close to that tight little warm body pitched his mind into overdrive. The very sexual side of him woke up and wanted to play. His amorous thoughts were smacked out of his head by her scream which bolted him straight up in the bed.

He cradled her in his arms as he held her close, whispering in her ear, "You are safe, you can sleep now."

Jacquetta slept better the following Saturday night than she had in years. Marriage to Orlando just might be the thing she needed. A reason to look forward to going to bed at night.

Chapter 6- The Incognito Wife

Orlando was all smiles as he began his Monday morning at Flynn Hardware. His brother, Woodson, noticed the pep in his little brother's step.

"So what is with the big grin little brother?" Woodson wanted to know.

"Just thinking about my weekend," he smiled as he continued to count the bags of seed and feed which arrived that morning.

Woodson was the oldest of the Flynn boys. He was 42, divorced, somewhat bitter and the father of three kids he rarely saw since his wife moved to Arizona with her new husband. He was thoroughly convinced every woman was a walking vagina with teeth that clamped down on a man's wallet. His ex-wife was the reason Woodson was a part-time employee of Flynn Hardware instead of the managing owner. Orlando had to buy him out to make certain Woodson's ex, Susan, didn't take his share of the company in the divorce.

The middle brother, Christopher, hated the hardware store: the smell, the nails and every seed in the building. He gave his share to Orlando with the understanding that he would never be asked to work in it, take inventory or even drive by the building. Christopher was a self-proclaimed ladies' man with expensive tastes, and an eye for nubile flesh. At 40 he had no intention of settling down anytime soon. He made his money by creating an app geared towards dating younger women who required financial sponsorship.

Every six months or so, he had a new young thing who needed some help with a car note, text book money or a spring break get away to decompress. The good thing, if one could consider Christopher's lifestyle a good thing, he was mainly interested in graduated students.

"The 18-23 year-olds are simply too young for my type of conversation," Christopher spouted. Yet, no matter what the tasks set before them, the brothers would all be on the same page. That was until now. They had no idea what Orlando was talking about. Well, that wasn't so unusual either. Their little brother was a different type of animal. He talked very little to either of them and when he did, he spoke in a very flat, monotone voice as if they were all hard of hearing or slightly daft.

"I need some help this week guys," he told his brothers. "I have a new shed being delivered this evening, and it is basically a small house. I need some assistance getting the foundation under it and getting it set up to catch the morning sun."

"What are you going to do with the shed, make a home gym or something?" Woodson asked.

"No, it's my wife's new studio. I go and pick her up on Friday, so I want to make sure I have all of that in place. I also want to add a fresh coat of paint to the dining room and living room, possibly the bedroom," he told Christopher. Although he and Jacquetta hadn't officially gotten married yet, he didn't want his family to know that detail. It also helped him to get it in his head that come Friday, he was going to be a married man.

Christopher laughed, "I don't do manual, but as a gift to you, I will get a couple of the kids from the college to come over and get it done on Wednesday. I will throw a few bucks their way."

"Thanks man that means a lot. I am going to go neutral so she has a fresh palette. If she wants the walls any other color, she will change them," he told his brothers with a huge grin. This was also a side of their little brother they didn't often see; Orlando smiling.

Woodson had heard about Becca, but didn't want to bring up the subject. "So, you ready for her to come to the house?"

"What do you mean am I ready? I am beyond ready. I am tired of those white walls and two rooms of furniture. I am ready to make that house a home. Who knows...next year this time, I may make you guys Uncles," he said with his eyes wide.

Mr. Pendergrast, a customer who came in once a week to buy a single nail or screw, walked into the store before either brother had a chance to respond to what Orlando had said. Christopher whispered, "So you think he is in denial?"

"I don't know what he is in...why is he putting a studio in the back yard...isn't Becca a teacher?"

"Maybe she is going to give private lessons or something...," Christopher said. "I mean, you think he is still going to marry her carrying another man's baby?"

"Beats the hell out of me...he said he hoped to make us Uncles next year. Becca is due this year. He has to be talking about someone else," Woodson responded.

"Who? He is always here at the store or wandering about

his house butt damned naked. I'm surprised no one has called the cops on his weird ass," Christopher said.

Woodson chuckled, "Let's stay positive. Maybe he has found a little weird woman that thinks his naked ways are cool and they are going to do naked yoga or Zumba in the studio in the back yard."

Christopher shuddered. "Yuck. Naked, hairy body parts doing downward facing dog...I just threw up a little in my mouth."

"Well save some of that energy for this evening while we set up her studio...whoever *her* is," Woodson said.

"We get to meet *her* on Friday, so he says," Christopher mumbled. "I wonder what she is like?"

"Probably some petite blond with big boobs... that seems to be his type," Woodson snorted. "Doesn't matter anyway. Women are all man eaters."

"So, are you planning to go gay or something Woodson?"

""I ain't that damned mad at women to want a stick of wood in my mouth!"

Christopher started to say, "What if you were the one..."

Woodson picked up a nail gun. "You don't want to die on the one day of the year that you actually walked into Flynn Hardware!"

The laughter continued into the evening as the hardware store was closed early to meet the delivery truck at Orlando's with the giant prefabricated shed. *Her studio had arrived.* As much as he was tempted to take a photo to send to Jacquetta, he wanted to wait to get her reaction in person. Harlan Flynn, the patriarch, had no intention of lending a hand, but fired up the grill to cook some burgers and dogs for dinner. It did his old heart good to see his sons in the big back yard working together to get the building at the perfect angle.

"The morning sun is critical," Orlando told them. "I pre-measured to make sure I have that window angled just right." When his calculations were complete, he stood inside the roomy shed and opened the main door and windows. The afternoon light was also perfect as he stood in three different locations to test the lighting.

"Perfect! She is going to love this," he told the men of his family. The country cottage shed was 16 x 36 with a loft for storage of canvases and supplies. It was the same color green as the exterior of the home and he had flower boxes added under the shed windows. His father helped cut open a slot in the outer wall to install a small AC unit for the summer time. *This building is as cute as my wife.* It had two large windows and a farm house style door with lots of floor space for her easel, a modeling sofa or a table for still life. "Yeah, she is going to love this!"

Harlan also knew about Becca. This worried him a bit, that his son was still interested in being with *that* woman. "Who is this *she* you keep talking about?"

Orlando was excited. "I'm talking about my wife. You guys will get to meet her on Friday. I know you are going to love her as much as I do." Again, he didn't want to tell his father that he was getting married on Friday. Knowing his family as he did, if it was something they would comment on and try to change in his life, they would. He spoke of

Jacquetta in the present tense as his wife to give them a few days to get used to the idea.

Harlan dropped his burger, the spatula and the cold beer he held in his hand. When did his son have time to get married? He was always at the store or at home walking around his house butt naked. "Son, have you found another nudist?"

"What?" Orlando asked. "I'm not a nudist!"

"You like to walk around with your twig and berries dangling in nature. That makes you a nudist!" Harlan said.

"No Dad, nudists like to be out in public with other nude people. I like to be in the privacy of my house, in a comfortable state...there is a difference," he told his father.

Harlan peered over at Woodson who chimed in, "Nudists!"

Christopher muttered under his breath, "Weirdo!"

Orlando walked over and threw his arm around his brother. "I'm your weirdo little brother and you wouldn't trade me for the world. Seriously guys, you are going to love my wife!"

Harlan asked, "Is she a nudist too? 'Cause if she is, I am never coming over here again! I am not eating dinner with body parts flopping all over the damned place."

"No, she is an artist," he told them with pride.

All three of the Flynn men said in unison, "Yep. She's a weirdo too!"

Chapter 7 —Weirdo Number 2

Jacquetta felt like a weirdo. There were so many things she had purchased for her home that had been placed in the storage unit, along with the tons of wedding presents she had received two years ago. They were hers and she had no intention of returning any of the gifts. She knew at some point she would actually get married versus showing up at the church to have no groom as it had transpired two years ago.

Nothing inside of her could make her hate Sebastian. He was a good guy, but she was simply not mentally healthy at the time. She wasn't really certain she was healthy now, but Saturday night, she had slept well knowing Orlando was at her side. Nothing was going to change the five days of her life which had been taken away from her by men who wanted to sell her like a piece of meat. The number of times she had been examined, fondled or probed with fingers and other items, she didn't even want to think about in her waking hours. In her sleep and subconscious was a different container of fish. Those events caused her night terrors. Even when she managed to catch a few hours of sleep, she always woke up the same way, screaming.

Friday night she had given Orlando a start because of things he didn't know. All of the years that he came to visit, or weekend trips they had taken, she always had a separate room. He never knew about the night terrors because she never told him, or anyone the details of what was done to her body by those men. She had never spoken of it and saw no reason why she ever should. The night terrors were a part of her life and waking up during the night had become a norm.

Saturday night she had not awoken once. She slept all night cradled against his chest. Warm, safe, and secure in his arms. It felt damned good. If for no other reason, that one was enough of an excuse to marry the man, so she could sleep with him. She would deal with the sex part later. Right now, her mind was focused on some deep REM sleeping.

They had never made it to her storage unit because she didn't want him to know she had a storage unit with enough furniture to fill their home. There were vintage pieces from her grandmother's mother, collectible pieces from her father's mother, as well as three sets of china, crystal from Italy, LLadro's, Hummel's and baby furniture. It was the baby furniture she didn't want him to see until it was unloaded.

Her mother had saved it for her. One of the empty bedrooms in the house would be set up as a nursery. That part made her feel like a weirdo. She only prayed that he wouldn't want to try to rush and fill the room with an occupant.

The week normally slumped itself through the days getting to Friday at a snail's pace, but by Thursday evening she was ready. The truck was loaded with everything from the storage unit and her apartment. She rented it ahead of time and hired a few men to load it up in the same order she had loaded it in her storage unit. The truck would be unloaded by room and the boxes were labeled. The rear of the truck held the baby furniture which would come off first. The other items going from the back of the house to the front with the living room items being the last thing off the truck.

Every piece of linen would need to be washed, scrubbed and possibly hung out to freshen. "I should have asked if he has a clothes line. I will definitely need one of those," she said to herself. Other items would need to be dusted and aired out. The items had been in storage from well over two years. Her life has been boxed up, labeled, and sealed off in that storage unit as well.

Tonight she sat alone in an empty apartment on an air mattress, waiting again for her hero to come rescue her from a less than desirable life. She pulled the blanket up around her neck as she curled into a ball on the mattress. *I have so many beautiful antique quilts and bedding.* She also had thick hand-dyed Persian rugs, Italian vases and French stemware.

Finally a home of my own to put them in.

She drifted off into a light sleep, happy that tomorrow she would become his wife. All of the gifts that had been given to her for a life with one man were now going to finally be put to use in a life with another. Life was funny. She was going to move into a house he had purchased to start a life with one woman that was going to be furnished and lived in by another.

Tonight she took a pill so she could rest all evening. She left out a simple white dress to wear to the courthouse in the morning. "I guess I am ready as I will ever be," she spoke softly.

"Tomorrow I will be Jacquetta Flynn."

Orlando arrived at 9:30 am in slacks, a tie and a bouquet of fresh flowers. "Good morning 'Quetta," he said with a big grin as he stepped through the door to an empty apartment.

His eyes were wide as he asked her, "What in the world?"

"I am already loaded and we are ready to roll once we hit the courthouse and make it official. I have the results of our blood tests here," she told him as she took the paper from her purse.

"We need to rent the truck..." he said as he looked at the small overnight bag she had and the air mattress container.

"I rented the moving van and the tow dolly for your truck," she said. "Everything is loaded and ready," she told him again.

"I guess there is nothing left but to hit the courthouse and make us man and wife," he said gazing deeply into her eyes. The butterflies were back in her stomach. *He is looking at me differently.* She found herself smiling at her fiancé. *My fiancé.*

She followed him out the front door as she locked the apartment and slipped the keys in the super's box on the first floor. Nothing was said as she allowed her GPS on her phone to guide him to the courthouse. *I am about to be Orlando's wife.*

In front of the Honorable George T. Peebles, she promised to forsake all others and keep only unto him, and he promised to love her in sickness and in health until death parted them. A nervous kiss was shared between the newly wed couple as he added a gold band to her engagement ring and she added a gold band with a diamond to his.

"You remembered my ring size?" he asked her.

She looked at his right hand. He still wore the ring she'd had custom made for him for a birthday present when she was stationed in Naples. His wedding band she purchased at a local jewelers. "I remembered the size," she told him as she slipped her hand into his. Papers signed, together they left the courthouse as newlyweds.

Twenty minutes later with his pickup hitched to the back of the rental truck, he climbed behind the wheel as she rode shotgun. "Let's head home Mrs. Flynn," he said as he gave the horn two toots to Ms. Bonner who had kept watch over the truck while they were gone.

Jacquetta had given the old lady a nice comforter set for the winter as well as her kitchen table. She waved at her surrogate guardian angel as they rolled past the high rise window. "I'm ready Mr. Flynn. Ready to head to Venture to begin a new venture," she told him.

Orlando beamed as he entered I-75 headed south. "I am almost afraid to ask what is in the back of this big ass truck." He handled the big truck as if he were driving his own pickup.

"It's our new life," she said as she stared out the front window. "I sure hope we don't get divorced any time soon because I sure would hate to have to repack all that stuff."

"No, you won't get rid of me so easy. You know what...I am excited to see how you are going to transform that house into our home," he said with a huge grin.

"I'm excited too," she smiled back at him. In truth she truly was ready for a new voyage. The one she had been on was wrought full of disappointments. She deserved some happiness and she was going to get it. Even if that meant starting over in a town that registered as a black dot on a map.

Venture, Georgia was going to be her new home.

Chapter 8- The Un-Named Wife

The newly married Flynn's arrived in Venture a little after four o'clock. Several times during the ride, she looked down at her hand and eyed her ring finger. *Yep. A little gold band to go with the diamond ring. I am married now. I am married to Orlando Flynn and moving to a small college town where people will probably call me a Negro or a colored gal.*

Orlando looked over at her and smiled, "No turning back now Mrs. Flynn; we are home." As much as Orlando loved the small college town, it was in every sense of the word, a small town. Word spread through the municipality like fire on dry brush. For that reason alone, instead of coming in on the primary road, he drove the back route to his house. The moment anyone saw the moving truck coming into town, the nosey townsfolk would follow it to see who was moving in and where. He wanted to keep his surprise quiet until the cookout next weekend.

Orlando turned down Butcher Street, made a right on Baker, then another left on Candlestick. He pointed to an old music hall. "That is the Roxy. It is a book slash comic book store. My friend Ethan and his wife, Janie, own it. They are good people. I think you will like her a lot. Maybe once we get everything settled, we can have them over for dinner."

Jacquetta couldn't remember the last time she had people over for anything, let alone a sit down dinner. The closest she had gotten to having guests was Ms. Bonner coming over to watch *Scandal*, eating popcorn and swigging the cheap beer she brought with her.

"That sounds great," she told him.

"The hardware store is on Main Street which runs through the center of town. There is a Walmart but no Target and if you want the mall, you will have to drive to Valdosta," he told her. "I called ahead to let my family know we were close. My brothers and cousins are going to help us unload the truck. More than likely, my Dad is going to supervise, which is his way of doing nothing but getting in the way."

The truck made a right onto Elm Street to rows of craftsman homes in varying shades of greens and blues. The whole street was monotone with the exception of vibrant plants and foliage which added pops of color to the perfectly manicured lawns. It was an idyllic scene. She could almost feel her paintbrush recapturing what she was seeing.

It was also easy to know which house was Orlando's because the front porch was loaded with people looking down the street for the truck. He pulled up in front of the house to several pairs of staring eyes which were all zooming in on her. Just based on his descriptions of his family over the years, she already knew who was who.

"I am going to unhitch my pick-up and the tow, then back the truck in so we can get it unloaded. Excuse my family if they ask you weird questions, or just be nosey," he told her.

The front porch was fantastic. It began with only four steps that went to the hardwood porch which was stained a deep redwood tone. *I can put colorful flowers in these planters on those end caps. The rocking chairs are going to look great on this front porch.*

First, I have to deal with the people standing on the porch.

Jacquetta inhaled slowly, and exhaled her doubts as she opened the door and slid down from the seat. The expressions on his family's faces confirmed her fear that he didn't tell them she was black.

You can handle this.

You got this.

She slung her overnight bag that held a change of clothing over her shoulder and walked up to the porch and addressed his father first, "Good afternoon, I am Jacquetta. I assume by the looks on your faces, Orlando didn't tell you I had long hair."

Harlan Flynn was many things, but tactful wasn't in his list of virtues. "Long hair? Hell he didn't tell us you were a Negro!" He said this with his finger pointing at her. Mrs. Flynn's cheeks pinked up, but Jacquetta stayed cool.

She reached out and grabbed his finger, shaking it like it was his hand. "I hope Orlando also told you that possibly next year we are going to give you some Negro grandbabies as well."

This made his mouth drop open even further as the two brothers snickered. She spoke to her mother-in-law with a warmness that she genuinely felt for the woman, based solely on the stories that Orlando had shared about his mother, she knew the woman was a great mom. "Mrs. Flynn, I look forward to trying that famous peach pie of yours," she told her as she shook her hand.

She moved down the row of family members, starting with the brothers. "Hello Woodson, it is nice to meet you. And I know you are Christopher," she said as she shook each of their hands. She moved to the cousins, "I know each of you based on his descriptions," she said.

She spotted the scar on the head on Beau. "That is the scar you earned swinging from the rope down at the pond and nearly bursting your head wide open, which makes you Beau," she said. The scrawny one, who Orlando said looked like a crackhead fresh out of rehab, was June Bug. The last one, Jimmy Ray, was married to a controlling woman who kept him on a strict schedule.

He promptly spoke up, "How long do you think this is gonna take? It's taco night. Dinner is promptly at six o'clock."

Jacquetta grinned at him. "I will have you home before then Jimmy Ray." To Orlando's family, she began to explain how the unloading could proceed so that everyone could get home and back to their families. "I really appreciate everyone being here to lend us a hand. The truck is loaded by rooms. The back rooms are first, moving to the dining room and living room. If we are not done by 5:30, I won't be offended if you want to get home to your Emma, Jimmy Ray."

They were all staring at her gape-jawed. Woodson couldn't contain himself any longer. "You aren't a weirdo are you?"

"I'm sorry...?" she said, blinking her eyes.

Beau spoke up, "He is asking if you like to walk around the house naked as a jaybird like your weirdo husband?"

She started to laugh. "Well no. I don't." She continued to laugh as her new husband walked up on the porch to stand next to her.

She turned her head to look at him and said, "Honey, it seems as if you forgot to tell your folks an important detail about me having long hair."

Orlando's eyes were wide as he exclaimed, "Long hair? Hell, I thought they were going to flip out over you being black!"

She smiled at his father. "There is nothing I can do about my skin color." In her head she ran an inner dialogue of what she wanted to say to him starting with "... *we's married now, and I's gonna move into the big house and give you some pretty little mulatto babies!*"

"What?" Orlando said, looking confused. "No one wants you to change the color of your skin! Least of all me!"

"Never mind. Can we order some pizzas and wings for dinner so we can feed all these wonderful people for coming over to help us?" she asked him.

"Sure," he told her.

"But first, can I take a walk through the house so I can visualize where everything goes to help get this done quickly?" she asked her husband.

He surprised her by sweeping her off her feet into his arms as Christopher opened the front door so he could carry his new bride over the threshold. Jacquetta giggled like a school girl as she wrapped her arms around his neck.

"Welcome home Mrs. Flynn," he told her as he gave her a quick kiss on the lips then lowered her feet to the beautiful hardwood floors.

"This is beautiful," she told him as she pulled away and went to the kitchen first. The kitchen was amazing with an island stove and bar stool seating facing a great room with a fire place. A large window was over the kitchen sink which looked into the back yard. The window allowed in lots of natural light.

The formal dining room was the perfect size. It could easily hold the dining room table, the buffet and the china cabinet without crowding the room. She peered into a large living room and guest bed room that would be perfect for a home office for Orlando. She wandered down the hall to find two full bathrooms and a water closet near the front bedroom.

The master bedroom was in the back of the house along with two other bedrooms. Jacquetta absolutely loved the recess ceiling but everything was painted beige. Even the master bathroom which had an odd smell but the garden Jacuzzi tub caught her eye along with the really large walk-in closet.

She was humming as she went into the closet with her bag and changed her clothing into jeans, a tee and pair of sneakers. When she came out, she found Orlando too had changed clothes.

"Let's do this!" she told him as they headed to the front room to meet his family.

The front door was propped open as she stepped onto the

porch, her hair in a ponytail, and her sleeves mentally rolled up. She announced to his family, "The truck is loaded from the rear to the front of the house. The boxes are labeled as to what goes in what room. It should not take us long to get everything off and in the house, by then the pizza should be here and we can eat some supper. Are we ready?'

They were all still staring at her with their mouths open. Jacquetta was in a great mood. She loved the house, "I will take that as a yes. Baby, will you order the pizza? I have some cash in my pocket to pay for it?"

Orlando got really close to her, one hand on her butt cheek while the other dug around in her pockets, making a show of holding her butt longer than he needed as he pulled out the cash. She gave him a look of 'really?' as he chuckled, patted her on the ass and headed to the kitchen. He dialed the pizza shop as she made her way to the back of the truck, freeing the padlock and climbing up to open the door. Woodson, finally able to move from the spot where he was rooted, helped with the ramps but froze again when he saw the crib and bassinet. He stared at her stomach, then looked at his brother, then back at her stomach.

"No, not yet Woodson. A lot of these pieces I inherited, so I am going to set up the nursery," she told him.

It took less than two hours to get everything off the truck and into designated rooms. Thick Persian rugs she had purchased in Iraq were rolled out on to floors. Her favorite rug sat under the dining room table, a handmade wood table her grandfather had carved out of the tree in her Grandma's back yard. The matching china cabinet looked regal in the room along with the buffet. *I will keep fresh flowers on the table.* The boxes of crystal that she had purchased in Switzerland were placed beside the cabinet alongside the silver her mother had given her.

Boxes of dishes and appliances, gadgets, goblets, cups, saucers and kitchenware were unloaded by cartons into the kitchen. The beautiful cherry desk that her Grandmother prized was in the home office along with the huge chair her grandfather hand tufted with matching fabric buttons. In the den, she rolled out a beautiful rug which matched the furniture Orlando already had in the room.

The last items on the truck were two rocking chairs for the front porch and her art supplies. "Orlando, where should I put my art supplies?"

He grabbed a box and said, "Follow me." With her easels in hand, she trailed him around to the back of the house. It didn't take her long to spot the shed. He had even planted Impatiens and Morning Glories in the flower boxes under the windows.

Jacquetta was rooted to the spot where she stood on a garden stone which read, "Jacquetta & Orlando, June 26, 2015." He opened the door of the studio and she lost it. Tears overcame her as her body racked from the force of her joy.

"This has got to be the most wonderful thing I have ever received in my life," she told him.

He sat down the box of paints and brushes and pulled her into his arms. "Now you know how I felt when you said yes to marrying me."

Jacquetta fell into his arms and held him tight. Her face was buried into his shoulder as he kissed the top of her head. She squeezed him snugly as she looked at the beautiful little workspace.

Harlan Flynn watched the scene as he rubbed his chin in bewilderment. "Now don't that just beat all, Maggie Mae?"

"Yeah, did you see all of that stuff she brought into the house? That stuff ain't cheap. That nap and pile on those rugs, and that handcrafted furniture..." She paused while watching Jacquetta cling to her son. She whispered, "...he seems to know his lady. Who would have thought a little shed in the backyard would get that kind of reaction?" Maggie Flynn said.

"You think they are going to be happy?" he asked his wife.

"Looks like they already are," she responded.

Beau walked out onto the back porch. "I bet she is a closet weirdo."

Christopher laughed as he spoke softly, "But man she is a looker and did you see that china cabinet! That thing is handcrafted, whoever made that furniture is an artist."

He looked over at his little brother hugging his new wife. "Pizza's here!"

Chapter 9 - Pseudonymous

The rental truck, now completely empty, sat in the driveway. Orlando knew by morning every warm body on his street would have seen it. "Hey Christopher, grab a slice and let's take this truck back," Orlando said to his brother.

Jacquetta's eyes were wide. "Are you going to leave me with your family?"

He gave her a smile and a quick hug. "They are your family too. The rental place is just down the road and we can save on a one day rental versus bringing it back tomorrow. Be back in a jiffy." He kissed her on the temple as he grabbed a slice and put it on a napkin.

Christopher watched how Jacquetta was clinging to Orlando, almost afraid to let go. Out of curiosity, he asked loudly, knowing it would keep the conversation going while they were gone, "How did you two meet?"

"I won her in a card game," Orlando said as he grabbed the keys to his truck, handing them to Christopher.

"You did not!" Jacquetta exclaimed. "You beat up four men and stole me." She started to chuckle, "Well, you really pounded that guy who was holding my dog collar."

"Yeah, that bastard deserved it," Orlando said. "Especially after he hit you!"

Maggie Mae's mouth was wide as everyone in the room stared at them. "Hold on a minute," Jacquetta said as she went into the office to locate a box marked *personals*. She tore it open and pulled out a very thick green binder that she'd use to display the scrapbook pages of photos of her and

Orlando.

She brought the large green scrapbook she'd made to the table and sat it on the edge. Uncertain of where the glasses and plates were kept, she began to open cabinets until she located enough dinnerware to serve the pizza. She found forks and passed out paper towels as his family thumbed through the binder.

She opened the boxes of pizzas and began, "Orlando always exaggerates each time he tells the story of how he rescued me from the sex traffickers." Every eye in the room popped up from the binder and zoomed in on her. She continued speaking as if she were sharing her favorite recipe for making the perfect chocolate chip cookie. "I was kidnapped by some Afghani rebels when I was on a mission in Iraq in 2010. I was assigned to NATO, but had come in to do some translations, evaluate some art pieces and collect some samples to take back to Italy for carbon dating."

At the kitchen sink, she washed her hands and began to plate pie slices and wings, passing down a plate and fork with each pie piece. "I had been moved around so much over a five day period, I was just about to give up hope of ever getting home, when I was pulled by my dog collar into a smoke filled room of men buying and selling women, girls, boys...I think I even saw a few sheep," she told them.

Woodson's mouth was moving back and forth as he listened with as much interest as he could since his attention was divided between getting the slice in his mouth and watching his brother's wife. They clung to her every word.

"And sitting at the table of these very dangerous, callous

men, was your son. The lone white man in the group of cut throats and thieves," she said with a sigh. Her gaze wandered out the back window to her painting studio. A smile crept into the corner of her lips. She continued as she used the ice maker on the fridge to add ice to the glasses.

"I didn't know NATO had a tracker in me, and Orlando had been sent to find me. I thank God for him. I had managed to not be hurt too badly during the five days, but I was prepared to fight and die if I had to before I allowed any of those men...to touch me." Her voice dropped off a bit. Beau had stopped chewing and looked at her as if she had grown horns.

"Well go on, what happened after that?" Beau asked impatiently.

"Yeah, what happened after that?" Jimmy Ray parroted with his thick Southern accent.

She continued as she handed Woodson a second slice and a glass of Coke. He was half-holding the binder. Jacquetta turned the page. "This is us in Afghanistan six weeks later." She pulled the photos from the album, passing them around the table as she explained to his family. "We had a lot of trouble getting me back to my unit. We had run into some more rebels and a dirty bomb full of shrapnel exploded, wounding Orlando in his right but cheek."

"So that's how he got them thar scars on his butt?" Jimmy Ray asked. Suddenly embarrassed that he'd seen the location of the scars, he lowered his head. "Well, he is naked everything I come over!" He said in his defense.

Jacquetta patted him on the hand as she continued the

story, "Every six months, even after I went back to Italy from my assignment in Afghanistan, Orlando would come and hang out for a weekend or a week. I was in Italy for three years, then I got out of the military and moved to Paris to hone my painting skills. This is us at the Louvre," she said as she showed them the picture.

She picked up another picture. "This is us in Pisa...and this one is from a weekend in Verona...and here we are in Santa Margherita Ligure right outside of Genoa. We had to go there because he wanted to have some of the salami..."

"So you are an artist?" Beau asked as he shoved a whole wing in his mouth and pulled out a clean bone.

"I am a painter, yes. I am also an art historian. I am thinking about possibly teaching a few classes over at the college once I get all settled," she responded.

Maggie Mae leaned forward on the table. "So... the rush in the wedding..."

"What do you mean?" Jacquetta asked.

"You and Orlando had to get married...?" She craned her neck forward with the word *had*.

Jacquetta's mouth formed a big O. "Ohhhh nooooo! I am not expecting!"

Harlan piped up, "We don't mean to pry, but on the porch you said grandbabies, and then the first thing off the truck was the nursery furniture...."

"The truck was loaded by rooms. The back rooms of the house first, and the nursery is going to be in the back of the house, next to our bedroom. I just thought it would make unloading the truck much easier. As you see it took only a couple of hours to unload and set up six rooms of furniture," she said.

Woodson spoke up, "Those are some amazing pieces of handmade furniture."

She nodded. "Yes, my grandfather was a furniture maker. He had a little shop right outside of Kennesaw. The nursery furniture his father also made. It has been handed down in the family for years. I am the last girl, so it came to me. We hope by next year, we can have a little one to go with the furniture."

Harlan was smiling at her.

Maggie was smiling at her.

Woodson watched her with curiosity.

Beau spoke up, "I just want to know if you are a weirdo too?"

Orlando was coming through the back door. "Why are you so obsessed with asking people if they are weirdos? You constantly asking that question Beau makes you the weird one!"

"Wow, that was fast," Jacquetta said as she placed two slices of pepperoni pizza on a plate for him with a glass of Coke.

"Small town," he told her.

"Speaking of small towns son, I was wondering if this whole quick marriage thing was because Becca is coming home next week?" Maggie Mae said.

He bit into the slice. "Oh is that next week?"

"Her Mama said she has a big surprise," Maggie said.

Orlando sipped at his Coke to wash down the greasy

chunk of pizza. "I wouldn't know anything about it. She and I parted ways five months ago."

Woodson sat up. "I didn't know that!"

Orlando's eyes were on Jacquetta. "It freed me up to be with the woman I love."

Her hand was on her chin as the weight of her wedding rings reminded her she was his wife. Her ring finger slid back and forth over her bottom lip as she stared back at him.

"But son, why the quick wedding if she ain't expecting?" Harlan asked.

"Because, I knew all of you would act as if I had done something wrong if I had brought her home as *anything* other than my wife. Woodson is bitter on women. Christopher is a man whore and I am not big on church. We kept it small and private, and here we are," Orlando said. Both Woodson and Christopher balked at his words.

"But son," his mother said, "You sure this doesn't have anything to do with Becca's surprise?"

Orlando stood up. "Seriously Ma, are you going to insult my wife by implying that I married her because of some crap about Becca? Look at my wife. Look around this house. Look at these photos. I have had a life with this amazing woman for almost six years. I finally got the balls to do something about it. I love Jacquetta and I am raising a family with her in this house. I get to go to bed every night for the rest of my life with this wonderful woman who agreed to be my wife and a mother to our children. Do you seriously think that Becca is in any thought in my head?"

Beau leaned back in the chair. "I know my mind has only

been on Jacquetta since she stepped out of that truck. Orlando, you are a lucky cuss!"

Orlando frowned at his cousin. "Shut up you meathead," he said to Beau.

Maggie Mae whispered to her husband, "This is going to be the talk of the town."

Harlan whispered back, "I think that was his intention."

"Well what do *we* do...what do *we* say...?" Maggie Mae whispered again to her husband.

Harlan looked at his wife. "There ain't nothing to say. He loves her, she loves him- they have all this history together...." Harlan whispered as he thumbed through the pages of the binder.

Woodson stood up, raised his glass and said, "Welcome to the family Jacquetta. If there is anything you need to help you get settled, let us know."

Glasses clinked and hugs were passed out as Jacquetta was accepted into the Flynn family. She watched her husband chat with his parents and brothers, but his words still clung to the air in the room. Some of his words still clung to her as well. She was beginning to wonder how much of what he said had been true.

Chapter 10 – I'm Only Human

The evening Jacquetta spent with her husband was the furthest idea of what she expected her wedding night to be. At a little after midnight, she awoke with a start, her body layered in a cold sweat, uncertain where she was. She turned in the bed to reach for Orlando but he wasn't beside her. Instead of calling out to him, she pushed back the covers, swinging her legs out of the bed until her feet made contact with the thick rug she had placed on the side of the queen sized bed. In her slippers, she started out of the bedroom towards the kitchen. Silently she prayed.

Please don't let him be doing anything freaky.

Please don't let him be doing anything freaky.

The search for her husband didn't take long. He was seated in the rocker in the nursery staring at the crib. His eyes were fixed, not glazed over, as if he were in deep thought. Jacquetta had found it strange that as much as he enjoyed sitting in his home naked, he didn't like to sleep that way. He wore pajamas to bed. The same pajamas he was still wearing.

"Orlando…?" she called his name.

Slowly his head rose to look upon her with distant eyes. "I was simply feeling the weight of my day," his voice was dry when he spoke.

"I sure hope you aren't thinking about going back on this marriage. There is no way in hell I am packing all of this stuff up and taking it back," she told him.

Orlando leaned back in the rocker, looking at her, but not

really focusing on her face. "You know...I was amazed how much of what I said to my parents was the actual truth. While I was in the Army...all of those missions, it was like I was a hunting dog trained on command to sniff out and go fetch. Each mission seemed like it was going to be my last. One thing I always kept in my mind and close to my heart...," he said as he looked up at her, "...was you. What we have has always been, I guess a kind of untitled love. I didn't come every six months to check up on you, I came because I needed you to hold onto keep me sane."

He ran his hands through his thick dark hair. "I didn't call in the marker because I wanted to save face. I called in the marker so you could save me."

Until this point, she was uncertain what to say. "...Save you..."

"I was hurting. Every time I found myself hurting, I would turn to you. All I needed was a little time in your light and I could go on..." he said through a thickness in his voice.

"...Now I have you. You are here. In my life. Jacquetta you are actually my wife. All those years, all those trips with me sleeping in one room craving your touch, afraid to ask for what I wanted. Afraid to ask you to love me... All these years and here you are, my wife, in my bed...and I still can't fucking touch you...!"

Panic filled her voice when she spoke, "You said you would give me time."

"I will give you all the time you need Jacquetta, but when a man wakes up with a hard on so powerful that it's about to poke a hole through the mattress, time is the last thing on his mind!"

He was yelling at her when he spoke. He softened his voice with his next words which hit her hard. "I was about to wake you and beg for an ounce of compassion, a squeeze, a tug, let a man hold a boob, something to give me some relief," he said in a lowered voice.

Jacquetta laughed.

"Are you laughing at my pain?"

"No. I understand, but I'm not ready for physical yet," she told him.

"In general or with me?" he asked.

She leaned against the door jamb as she clenched and unclenched her fists. "I never told you the reason why Sebastian didn't show up to the wedding," she said to him as she shifted her position against the door jamb. She inhaled softly as she spoke to him, "A week before the wedding he decided to stay the night. I don't know why he thought it would be a good idea to wake me up all sexy like...with his fingers, you know..."

She wiped away a tear that ran down her cheek. "It's my fault really. I should have told him what happened to me on day three of my kidnapping, but I had some new meds that helped me sleep all night. The night terrors were gone, or at least I thought they were until I woke up to the feeling of fingers inside me..."

"What happened Jacquetta?" he asked her.

She wrapped her arms around herself as she stepped inside the room. "I tried to kill him, Orlando, that's what happened. By the time he snapped me out of it, I had nearly gouged out his eyes." He sat motionless in the chair watching her.

"I have found, that I do have feelings for you in that way but I am not ready, not just yet. I need a bit of time to get adjusted to all of this," she told him.

"Jacquetta I know, but I can't help but want you. It has been a while for me, and I can train myself, create the discipline, but that is also going to take some time. I mean, I can't...shit, I don't know what to say right now," he told her.

"Hold on," she said as she left the room. He could hear her rambling about in the closet in the other room. She came back with a pump bottle of body lotion, a hand towel and her iPod. The lotion and hand towel she gave to him, the iPod she strapped to her arm.

Orlando knew better than to say anything as she unbuttoned her pajama top and tied the ends under her ribcage. The pajama bottoms she removed and stood before him in a pair of black undies. Her eyes never met his as she thumbed through the songs on the device, finally settling on the one she thought was perfect.

Jacquetta turned her back to him and squatted down on the floor. One leg was extended as the music started. She began to flex her right butt cheek making it bounce to the rhythm of the music she had plugged into her ears. Slowly the left butt cheek joined the party as her butt cheeks moved one at a time.

Orlando's eyes were transfixed as he watched his wife move to music he could barely hear. She popped up on her feet to a standing position then back down to a squat. The firm, rounded butt cheeks still moving independently to an unheard beat. He watched, mesmerized as Jacquetta came to a standing position, bent over, grabbed her ankles, and her butt cheeks began to clap. Orlando almost forgot to breathe as he watched the private show she was putting on only for him.

Her hands touched the floor as her body weight leaned on to bent elbows until she was in a handstand, her hips gyrating in the air.

"Dayuuummm," he yelled as his hand fumbled to find the lotion bottle. He pumped a handful of lotion into his fisted palm, as a bit of drool ran down the side of his lip. Her hips pulsated in the air for four or five good pumps, gyrating, pumping, gyrating, and pumping again before she straightened her legs into a mid-air split.

His hand worked furiously as he watched his wife lower her body to the floor. Jacquetta was still in the splits as her ass cheeks bounced independently as she raised and lowered her butt while she bounced on the floor.

"Shiiiiiiiit," he yelled out as he collapsed in the chair, spent.

The song ended and Jacquetta slowly stood up from the floor, untied her pajama top and refastened the buttons. She said nothing to him as she pulled her pajama bottoms back on. "I'll meet you in the middle," she told him as she turned to make her way back to the bedroom.

"Jacquetta....that was frickin' awesome!" he huskily worded while still sprawled out in the chair, his right knee bent, his left leg extended. "I love you so much...." he said with a weak voice.

"I love you too Orlando, now come on to bed," she smiled at him.

"Okay," he said sheepishly. His legs felt like limp noodles as he rose, bringing the soiled washcloth to the hamper. There was no doubt in his mind that he was going to sleep a whole lot better tonight.

Chapter 11- Good Morning

The smell of coffee brewing and the sound of sausages sizzling pulled Jacquetta out of a groggy sleep towards the kitchen. Orlando fully dressed, standing over the stove, with his face almost glowing as he turned over the sausage patties in the pan. He took a carton of eggs from the fridge, along with heavy cream, cheese, scallions and mushrooms. Jacquetta said nothing as she watched him break the eggs and beat them in a bowl with some of the heavy cream. He poured the concoction into a second pan on the stove burner while tossing in the other ingredients. The man was humming as he scrambled the eggs in the pan. A new found happiness emitted from him which was nearly tangible as he began to plate the breakfast. He looked up to find her standing there watching him.

She asked him, "Is it possible to get a cup of whatever it is that you are feeling while you are cooking those eggs?"

He winked at her. "You can have as much of this as you'd like. This morning, let's just start with some coffee and breakfast."

The plates were brought to the table as she joined him. Furtive glances were shared between them until he finally broke the silence, "I don't care where you learned how to do that thing you did last night, nor do I want to know, but promise me that when I am a good boy, you will do it for me again."

Jacquetta nearly choked on her coffee. "Funny, when you are a good boy...funny...."

"I mean seriously, any time I come home with jewelry, flowers, or I cook dinner, works pretty damned well for me too. I tell you...I ...wow." He leaned over and kissed her forehead. "Thank you. I will cherish that gift you shared with me."

"And I got breakfast out of the deal as well," she said over the mug of steamy hot coffee.

"No, I feel guilty because I forgot to tell you I have to work today. I am off tomorrow and Monday, which are my normal free days," he said as he forked eggs into his mouth.

"I take it the hardware store is pretty close by?" she wanted to know.

"Yes, out the front door, take a left, go down four blocks to Main, make a right, come up two blocks and you can't miss it."

"Okay, it's not a problem. I have a lot to unpack, wash and get put away today, so I will be fine. This is a lovely home. I am so happy all the furniture goes really well with the house," she told him.

"Yeah, everything seems to be falling into place." Orlando looked down at his watch. "Ooh, I gotta run. Tomorrow, let's talk honeymoon, your car, and details okay?"

"Sure," she said to him.

He kissed her on the forehead again. "I will be home about sixish. The number to the store is on the wall calendar. I have my cell too."

"I will be fine. Go... make that money," she told him as she swatted him on his bum.

He made it to the front door before looking back at her. "I am so glad you are here."

Her response was honest, "I'm glad I am here too."

"See ya later," he told her.

"I'll be here," she responded.

Alone.

She sat at the table long after she finished her breakfast. A second cup of coffee was in order as she looked about the one level craftsman home. The rugs she laid last night really warmed up the space and if there were some color added to accent walls, the house would be a real showstopper.

Our home.

It didn't take her long to wash up the few dishes left over from breakfast, shower, do a couple loads of laundry and remake the beds with her nice linens. Her grandmother's eyelet sham was used in the guest room on her old bed along with a pretty mint green matelassé coverlet. She snapped a picture of the coverlet to get a quart of paint for the wall behind the bed.

Next she moved to the master bedroom. The whole room smelled like dude. She checked the hamper and nothing much was in it. The bathroom held no sour towels or damp bath mats, but it had a funk to it that she didn't care to live with. In the box labeled bedroom, she found some candles that she placed on the bureau and lit. Within minutes a warm aroma filled the room which also filled her with a new sensation.

Longing.

Her body wanted...needed...craved....*my husband?*

That's a weird feeling.

Even stranger, she had a need to see him.

Her bicycle leaned against the back porch from where Christopher had perched it last night. It had a nice sized basket on the handlebars and rack above the back tire. She would use it to go for a ride down to Flynn's Hardware. Jacquetta blew out the candles in the bedroom. Quickly she ran down the hall and checked the fridge to get a bottle of water where she found his lunch bag. Her set of house keys hung on the hook by the back door, which she grabbed along with Orlando's lunch that she tossed into the basket, and off she pedaled. She rode past two-level craftsman homes. She rode by ranch styled homes. The yards were meticulously groomed with colored rocks, colored mulch and vibrant colorful flowers. Four blocks down the sidewalk she pedaled, waving at neighbors on porches who waved back to her. Several even stopped her to ask who she was and where she was headed. They were pleasant people who were kind and welcoming to her as she bid them farewell and continued towards the store. At the corner of Sycamore and Main, she made a right and bicycled up the road until she spotted the building.

It looked exactly like a Norman Rockwell painting of any hardware store in small town Americana. The building even had a cigar Indian out front along with colorful flags, flowers, and piles of fertilizer for sale. Busy people were coming and going from the building with smiling faces and little brown bags of goodies to do home repairs and projects. Jacquetta needed a padlock for her studio, paint for the master bath, and that mint green paint for the accent wall in the guest bedroom.

That can be done on Tuesday.

I can paint the bathroom on Wednesday.

Maybe paint an accent wall in the master bedroom on Thursday.

I am thinking of tiling the backsplash in the kitchen.

Oh dear God, I am nesting.

A grin covered her face as she pushed open the door of Flynn Hardware and stepped inside with her husband's lunch in her hand. Jacquetta was greeted by a really tall, well built, good-looking black man.

"Hey there. I'm Rodney, what can I help you find today?"

Jacquetta shared with him the list of items she needed. As they walked and talked, it occurred to her that Rodney was trying to ask her out. Her ring finger was shielded by Orlando's lunch bag.

"There isn't much to do in Venture, but there are some nice jazz clubs and restaurants in Valdosta," he said as he showed her padlocks for the shed.

"Thank you, I will keep that in mind," she told him.

Rodney had a 100-watt smile. That body of his had muscles on top of muscles and a nice tapered waist, if a girl was into that kind of thing. He moved a step closer as Jacquetta moved a step back. "I am trying to ask you out Ms...."

She didn't smile at him. "I understand. However, I am taken and it is Mrs..." She held up her ring finger.

He was not giving up. "Mrs...can I get your name?"

This is where she did give him a small smile as Harlan came around the corner. "I am Jacquetta," she told him as she offered a handshake. "Jacquetta Flynn."

The look of surprise on his face only multiplied exponentially as she called out to Harlan, "Hey Dad! How are you doing today?"

Harlan reacted as if he had been hit in the ass with a cattle prod. His back went rigid as beet red color crept up his neck. The sound of her voice brought Orlando around the corner as well, grinning as he embraced his wife, planting a sloppy wet kiss on her cheek.

"Stop teasing my dad 'Quetta," he told her.

"Well, at some point he will have to get used to having a Negro daughter-in-law," she said with a chuckle.

Orlando wasn't as amused as he focused in on Rodney, who was still standing there staring. "Rodney, were you hitting on my wife?" The man started stuttering. "I have told you more than once, stop hitting on the female customers. If they are interested in you let them make the first move. You are going to get me sued!"

He turned his attention to Jacquetta. "What do I owe the honor of this visit from my beautiful wife?"

She held up the lunch bag. "You forgot your lunch."

"You rode your bike all the way down here to bring me my lunch?"

"That...and you forgot to properly kiss me before you left this morning," she said as she wrapped her arms tightly around his waist.

"Oh, I can fix that quick, fast and in a hurry," he said as

he lowered his head. His lips touched hers and a spark ran down her right leg making it twitch. Orlando pulled her closer to him to where she could feel all the maleness of him against her body. A body that was heating up and responding.

She opened her mouth a little as his tongue slipped inside, toying playfully with her own, and then he stopped. In her ear he whispered, "It would seem as if somebody is getting thirsty; but I'm not judging." He said this with a twinkle in his eye.

Her throat was dry as she pulled away from him, swallowing hard. She whispered back, "We are getting there. A few more kisses like that, and girl is gonna whip out a 10-gallon pitcher to drink her fill."

All eyes were still on them as he looked at his employees in the store. "I am certain we have customers who need some help." He turned to his wife. "You, I will assist personally."

Jacquetta fanned herself with her paper note before she handed him her list on the index card. The pride which her husband exhibited in his family's store was a wonder to her as she cooed and fawned over everything that he was excited to show her. In her mind, she was already repainting several of the walls with a fresh coat of white paint, adding a few murals of people using the products they bought in the store. As his wife, she also felt pride that her man was happy with his job and his life. She wanted to keep it that way, not only for him, but for herself as well.

We both deserve some happiness.

Chapter 12- Unrecognizable

The early rays of the morning sun peeped through the curtains of the bedroom as Orlando rolled over to find himself alone in bed. He could smell the coffee brewing in the kitchen but didn't hear any meat being cooked. Initially when he had awakened, he was uncertain where he was because everything smelled so different. Even the odd smell in the bathroom was gone.

He arrived home from work last night to find a lot of small touches added to the house. The beds had been made-over with new linens and he could feel the difference in the sheeting. The master bath had new rugs and shower curtains and touches to it that weren't too girly or too masculine, but a shared space of two people. He liked sharing space with Jacquetta.

My wife.

Last night, she only woke once. She was in a cold sweat again, but he only laid his hand across her abdomen to calm her, and soon she fell back to sleep. He understood the night terrors. Those he understood all too well. What bothered him about hers was that she still had not spoken about what happened to her on day 3 of her captivity.

She will tell me when she is ready.

Wearing his pajamas, he strolled down the hall to the kitchen to find her out back with a cup of coffee, potting a plant. Instead of bothering her, he went out the front door, morning cup of coffee in hand to get the Sunday paper. Mrs. Marvin was on her way to church as she threw up her hand to wave to him.

"Morning Orlando. Nice to see you in some clothes! Say howdy to 'Quetta for me and let her know to get those bulbs I gave her in the ground as soon as possible," she said loudly.

The neighbor who lived to the left of them was Guy Pearson. He was an all-around asshole that rode on Orlando's last nerve. If there was ever a living example of a Grinch, that man was the personification of Grinchdom. He raised his hand and waved to Orlando.

Orlando looked over his shoulder to see if Guy was waving at someone else. Then Guy waved again. This time beckoning Orlando to come over.

Again, Orlando looked over his shoulder to make sure the crotchety bastard was talking to him. "I'm talking to you Dingleberry! Get over here!" Guy yelled at him.

He had not put on any slippers when he came out to get the paper, his feet were bare as he made his way across the thick Bermuda grass to the property line where Guy's brown grass started. "Hey, those lamb chops 'Quetta cooked last night were fantastic. You are luckier than you need to be you little butt smear, but that wife of yours...hubba hubba! And she can cook too!" He handed Orlando a ten dollar bill.

Orlando was too stunned to even respond to the man.

Guy waved him off. "Give that to my 'Quetta and tell her I said thank you. I am feeling much better," Guy said as he made his way back to his porch. "Don't think that this makes me like you any more since you married up, dickhead! I do like that wife of yours, though. Maybe she can talk your weird ass into keeping on some clothes or hanging some curtains. I get sick of seeing your naked buttocks every time I go to look out my window…."

He was still mumbling as he walked away.

Confused and uncertain of what just happened, he looked down the street. Neighbors who saw him every day but never spoke, were waving to him as they headed off to church or to start their Sunday morning.

What in the hell?

"How does everybody on this street seem to know you?" he asked his wife as he came around the backside of the house.

"A black lady riding a bike through the neighborhood catches people's attention. I stopped, introduced myself, and everybody wanted to know the same thing," she said. He waited for her to continue. "They wanted to know if I would be successful at getting you to put on some clothes."

He watched her with interest as she opened the back door to let herself in the house and pour herself a second cup of coffee. Jacquetta removed the smock she wore to pot the plants and hung it in the laundry room. She scrubbed her hands and under her nails in the utility sink as he stood there staring at her.

"Let's try this again. Good morning," she said as she walked over to kiss him on the cheek. "I'm not really a breakfast person. Coffee, peanut butter toast and a banana can carry me for the morning, but I made some oatmeal. Here have a bowl. I cut up an apple, added some raisins, walnuts and brown sugar."

The plant she had potted outside now sat in the middle

of the kitchen table. He noticed the other plants in the house as well. There was even one by his Big Daddy chair that also had a new cushion in it. "What's with the cushion?"

"That's for your naked butt. If we have company and someone else has to sit in the chair, I can remove the cushion and no one will be subjected to your ass spores," she said with a grin.

"Funny...really funny," he said as he looked at the healthy bowl of mush.

I don't want this crap.

I want some meat and eggs....

As if she read his mind. "Your body will appreciate not having greasy fried meats and cheese-loaded eggs every day. Besides, you don't want to have a coronary and leave all of this sexy to be cared for by Rodney."

He wasn't smiling. "Yeah, I knew he was hitting on you! I am going to fire him."

"Oh stop it. He didn't know who I was until I told him," she said as she encouraged him to eat his breakfast. "What is the plan for today?"

He spooned in a mouthful of oatmeal and swallowed, frowning as the slimy, mushy grains slid down his throat. "I normally go over to my parents for Sunday dinner. Me, my brothers and Dad watch a game, or work on a project or something like that...I cut the grass in the afternoon before going over. That's it."

"Okay, and the normal plan for Monday's..."

"I sleep in, then meet my buddies for afternoon golf. I have a tee time at 2 pm," he told her.

"Okay, so that leaves me Sunday's... anything before grass cutting and your parents, and the time slot on Monday before 1:30..." she said aloud as she made a note in her Happy Planner.

"When you say it like that..." he mumbled.

"Like what Orlando? I can't show up and change everything in your life. You need downtime as well. If Sunday dinner at your folks is always on the schedule, then I need to call Mrs. Maggie Mae and find out what to bring. I was planning to bake a cake today anyway...," she told him.

"A cake would be great. My Ma makes great pies but she can't cook a cake worth shit," he said.

That was all Jacquetta needed to hear. She turned on the stove and started pulling out the sugar, flour, eggs, butter, milk, baking soda and her fancy red mixer. He already had eggs and sugar since he seemed to live on the two items. The rest of the stuff his wife was pulling out to make the cake, he wasn't sure where it came from.

"When I left the hardware store I went over to Smollet's Market to pick up a couple of things. I didn't like their meats though, which is why I went to the butcher shop. Mr. Baldwin says 'hello'. He gave me a great deal on those lamb chops we had last night," she told him.

Orlando watched with interest as she measured, poured, and set aside the flour. She began to cream the eggs and sugar, adding a bit of vanilla, and some other flavor into the mix.

"You are making a cake from scratch?"

"Well, not from scratch because I have everything I need to go in it," she told him as she cracked the eggs allowing them to slide into the mixer.

He thought about the ten spot in his other hand. "Before I forget - here. This is from the talking, venom spitting troll next door. He wanted to thank you for the lamb chops last night," he told her.

"Oh that was nice of him." She took the ten and stuck it in a jar in the kitchen cabinet. "Butter and egg money," she laughed. From under the cabinet she pulled out three baking pans. Her hands were nimble as she greased and floured each and set them aside. She was still talking to him as she grabbed a lemon from the fridge and began to scrape the zest to go in the batter.

Orlando didn't want to make the comparison, but Becca couldn't follow the directions to bake a cake from a box. Jacquetta was making one from a recipe inside of her head. He forgot all about the oatmeal as he watched his wife finish the batter and fold it into the pans. He truly enjoyed the sight of her bottom as she bent over to slide the cake pans in the oven. A couple of buttons were pushed as she set the timer on to monitor the cooking time on the cake rounds.

"You did a lot yesterday with only a bicycle. If I had known I would have left you my truck. Tomorrow, we will go to the dealership and find you a good used car," he said as he watched her perfect little butt bend over to put the mixer under the counter.

"Yeah...about that....uhm, I don't want a used car," she told him.

"I can swing a small car note, I have a nice down payment for it, but I still have a year to pay on my truck. In the colder months, sales slump off at the store, so any fat stores I have in the bank are to tide us over in the slower months," he said.

Jacquetta breathed deeply as she came around the island. "I know as my husband you feel like you have to take care of everything. You don't."

She rubbed his arm with the tips of her fingers as she prepared herself to tell him a partial lie. "I have been saving for a while, and I have enough to get me a new, moderately priced SUV. I can get a new one for maybe twenty-two," she told him.

"You sure...you don't have to spend all of your money on a car," he told her.

"I'm not, but I don't have to pay rent anymore either. Speaking of that, I can take over payment of the utilities. I sold a few paintings, so I have some cushion."

Orlando didn't want to admit his ego was bruised. He wanted to be able to get her the car as a gift. A new one was out of his budget, but he could have swung the cost of a really good used one. He had even picked out a few for her to choose from. "No, why don't you put that towards our honeymoon."

"Oooh, honeymoon. Where do you want to go? I would love to go somewhere in the Caribbean," she said.

"Jamaica, Puerto Rico...," he suggested.

"Aruba! Or maybe Turks and Caicos!" she said.

"Sure. Do you need me to help plan it?"

"No, I just need the days that you can go on vacation, and I will do the rest," she grinned.

"Okay," he said watching the joy on her face. She was truly a special woman. He wasn't sure what she did to charm the old goat next door or how she met all of his neighbors, but she was a force in which to be reckoned. It was one more thing that he loved about the woman.

"Hey Husband. I would like to hang some of these paintings today before we head over to your parents," she told him as she pulled out the level and hammer. "Can we do that?"

"I will get right on that as soon as I swallow this bowl of mush," he said with a grimace.

Jacquetta kissed his cheek before she made her way down the hall to collect the paintings she wanted hung in each room. The house was going to be very nice when she finished it, of this she was certain.

Chapter 13 - Innominate

The Sunday afternoon family dinner turned into an informal reception. Orlando & Jacquetta arrived at the Flynn family home to find everyone from the family's church, Orlando's business associates and even a few of his neighbors had stopped by to congratulate the couple and meet the new wife. A few of the people were plain ole' nosey and came by to take a gander at the black girl that Orlando brought home last week. Others wanted to check to see how pregnant she was because of the sudden wedding. A few rumors had spread and others wanted to meet the sassy black woman who looked a lot like one of the kids on the eighties sitcom show about the upper class black family.

A little old lady with a large flower in her hair pulled Jacquetta to the side, "I hate to be nosey, but what was it like working on a television show? Is he that funny in person?"

Jacquetta politely explained to the woman that she was not a grown up Rudy Huxtable. A sad sigh went across the group of ladies perched in the corner as the little old lady yelled out, "She ain't nobody famous! Elmira, you need to put on your dang gone glasses. She ain't no grown up Huxtable kid!" Orlando only smiled at her from across the room before he was cornered by a few of the menfolk.

The butcher, the baker and the banker wanted Orlando to explain why his wife was riding through the neighborhood doing her shopping on a bike. "You can't afford to get your wife a car? As pretty as she is, she don't need to be developing big ole muscled legs or anything," Mr. Smollett the owner of the grocery store told him.

Mr. Baldwin, the butcher, wasn't getting left out of the conversation. His piebald head looked like a Rorschach print as he ran a white cotton hanky over his sweaty scalp. "If you need a few dollars we can start up a collection to help you make the down payment. I mean I could have loaded her up with good deals yesterday, but she barely had room in her little basket for the lamb chops I sold her!"

Orlando was looking for an escape. None was to be found as Courtney Rogers, the manager at the local franchise bank came over. He took pride in telling the men, "You old fussbudgets need to mind your own business. You know nothing about the state of these young people's affairs."

"Thank you Courtney," Orlando said.

"You are welcome. The two of you should really come see me about investments, estate planning and setting up a trust for your children," he told Orlando.

This confused him a bit as he thought about what was in his personal accounts as well as the business accounts. He had banked with that branch for many years and knew Courtney personally. The man had never offered him any financial advice, which was odd, especially with him doing so now.

The thing that was even stranger was Guy Pearson being in his parent's kitchen eating a piece of his wife's cake. *I haven't even tried her cake yet.*

His face was stern as he made a beeline for his neighbor, but Jacquetta stopped him. "You look angry Orlando, what is going on?"

"Who invited his mean ass? He has some nerve sitting in here eating your cake! I haven't even had a sample of it yet. I don't even know what your cake tastes like!" Orlando said with a poked out lip.

She stood on her tiptoes as she whispered in his ear, "Is that some kind of sexy double entendre?"

Orlando's eyes went from Guy down to his wife, then back over to Guy. Slowly coming back to Jacquetta's face. He was trying not to smile, but he couldn't help it. "That is not what I meant 'Quetta," he said with a smirk.

She didn't let it go. Her eyebrows went up. "Oh, you don't want to know how yummy my cake tastes or how moist it is when it almost melts in your mouth."

Orlando stepped back and thumped her on the arm. He was scowling when he told her, "That is just plain mean. What's worse is that you are going to have me terrifying all these little old ladies in the room when my trouser snake starts to move and wiggle in my pants."

"Your *what?*" She said as she burst into laughter.

He pulled his wife into his arms. Speaking directly into her ear, "Yeah, you had your eyes closed when you were doing that little dance. You should have looked back to see my mighty cobra in ready mode. It is an impressive instrument."

She pulled away from him as the goosebumps began to prickle her arms. Jacquetta started to fan herself as she walked away, with a bit of a swish in her step as he watched her. "Come on over here man and get some of my cake before it's all gone," she said. She sliced him off a decent piece, plated it on a saucer and sat it on the table.

By the seat next to Guy.

Guy, whose cake was all gone.

Guy, who stuck his fork into Orlando's cake before he even had a chance to taste it. "You don't deserve any cake you naked weirdo," Guy said to him as he lobbed off half of the slice.

Orlando was about to sock him, until Guy whispered, "If you hit me, I'm going to tell my 'Quetta on you!"

"How the hell did she get to be your 'Quetta? You just met her yesterday you old diaper stain!"

"I'm going to keep a close eye on her while you are at work you tart little butt pad," Guy hissed at him.

Orlando leaned over, picking up the back half of the cake and bit off a big chunk. "I get to have this and any other yummy piece of heaven she chooses to make me. Just for that you nasty bladder bag, I am going to personally bring you a plate of dinner, to make sure you spend the night holding your bloated belly as you fart out shards of brown anger."

Guy leaned in and got closer to Orlando. "Yes and I am going to encourage my 'Quetta to support your nakedness by joining in on your little game, you candy ass fart muncher."

"I can't stand you, you shit stain on humanity," Orlando hissed at him through tight lips.

"I have the same amount of love for you, you walking, talking, bad driving, piece of constipation," Guy whispered back.

They were smiling at each other when Jacquetta came back to the table. "It is so good to see you both getting along. Orlando, Guy said that if there was ever anything I needed, he would be willing to lend me a hand."

Orlando had started to turn red as the neighbor from hell winked at him. "I sure will Ms. 'Quetta. While he is at that store all day and night, you can count on me to lend you a hand."

The movement was so quick that for a second Jacquetta had a flashback to Abu Dhabi. Orlando was up and had the man by his collar and on his feet. The chair didn't even scrape the floor. He turned Guy's body as he draped his arm over the man's shoulder and guided him to the front door, saying very loudly, "Thank you for stopping by Guy. It is so good to see you." He physically pushed the man out of the door onto the front porch holding him by the collar and whispered in his ear, "If I ever catch you in my house, I am going to put a bullet in you and act like I had a flashback to Kandahar, you pig smelling snout sucker!"

Jacquetta wanted to say something, but Jimmy Ray had emptied a pickle jar, dried it out with his tee shirt and sat the jar on the counter to collect donations for the newlyweds.

"Right over here, errrybody!" Jimmy Ray called out. "If you want to drop some good will into the jar for my cousin and his new wife, come on over. I can tell you, they don't need any furniture or dishes. She came with errrrythang a girl could want in a house, but she sure needs a decent car!"

Orlando sat down in the chair, completely defeated. Jacquetta plopped down in his lap. They both watched in disbelief as Jimmy Ray put his white tee back on, only now it had green streaks of dampness on it from the pickled vinegar in the jar. He spent the rest of the evening smelling like a dill pickle. Family, neighbors, friends and well-wishers all passed by the jar, dropping in whatever was in their pockets or purses. Even Harlan added a few bills to the jar.

"Gee thanks Dad!" Jacquetta called out.

Harlan's butt cheeks tightened up faster than a nun at a hoedown. The red crept up his face as he looked at her with shock and surprise.

"Stop scaring my Dad 'Quetta," Orlando told her again.

"Baby, I am not going to get any lighter. If anything, when we get back from Aruba, I am going to be darker. You know, even more Negro," she said with a chuckle. "Maybe I should kiss you with some tongue while he is over in the corner staring at us."

"Maybe you should kiss me with that tantalizing tongue because you want to," he said in a low husky voice. It was the way he said it that made her look at him in a way she had never done until this moment. She looked at him as her man.

There was no mistaking the look because Orlando understood the significance of the gaze as he sat up in the chair. His hand was still around her waist with his fingers pressing against her butt cheek. Fingers, firm and strong touched the back of her neck, going into her hair and pulling her face to his. The first touch of his lips were soft, almost exploratory, as he deepened the kiss between them. Her knees came into his lap as her hands went up around his neck, running her fingers into his hair, pulling him closer.

Maggie Mae brought the kiss to an end. "You two do that at your own house. Come on over her Jacquetta, I want you to meet some of the ladies in my quilting bee!"

He pointed at her as she walked away. She knew what the point meant, but just to make sure, he appeared at her side a few minutes later with an ice cold glass of water. She turned and laughed out loud, as she raised her glass to Harlan, "Salud! Dad!"

Her father-in-law twitched again like someone had run up behind him and screamed boo! She knew she shouldn't do it, but at some point he was going to have to get used to her. Jacquetta wasn't planning on going anywhere. The town was embracing her and she it.

For the first time in a long time, she felt like she had a home.

Chapter 14 – X Marks the Spot

Both Orlando and Jacquetta were pooped by the time they reached home. The cake was all gone and six people wanted the recipe. She promised tomorrow she would email it to several ladies, and somehow she was now a member of a recipe swapping club. This was Maggie Mae's idea after Guy was gushing over her daughter-in-law's lamb chops. One taste of the cake and her mother-in-law wanted all her recipe secrets.

I don't have a lot of secrets.

Except for the feelings that were secretly consuming her thoughts about her husband. He was an exceptional kisser. She liked kissing him and wanted to do so again, but they were adults.

Hell, we are married.

Kissing leads to other stuff, which I used to enjoy, but I haven't been able to in years.

She tried not to sneak a peek as he undressed and walked around the bedroom bare. He even went back to the kitchen to get some water wearing nothing more than a smile. Orlando Flynn had a nice bum and an even better body. He had that long dark hair, wide, muscular shoulders, a broad, hairless, muscular chest, and strong thighs. The man was in great shape for someone nearing 40 years old. At 33, she knew she needed to get started having a few babies if it was going to happen in this lifetime.

I want to have his babies.

I want this life with him.

She hadn't noticed that he was back in the bedroom and turning down his side of the bed. She sat on her side, gazing out the window, trying to figure out how to say what she wanted to tell him.

"Maybe if you went ahead and spit out, versus bandying it about in your head, it would help you work through it," he told her.

"I wasn't aware I spoke out loud," she muttered.

"You didn't. I read your face," he told her as he pulled on his pajama bottoms. He lowered his voice an octave as he lay his head on the pillow watching her, "Tell me what you need Jacquetta."

"I need you to kiss me some more. You are really good at it," she said as she slid into the bed.

"We are in bed - so no," he said flatly.

"What do you mean no?"

"Just what I said. I only have so much strength. Kissing you in a room full of people is one thing. Kissing you in this bed, tonight, is another. Good night," he told her as he reached over to turn off his lamp.

The lamp on her nightstand was still on. She moved closer to him. "How do you expect me to build up my thirst if you won't let me run and play?"

"You are getting thirsty, but I am damned near dehydrated, so ain't no running and playing for me," he said flatly.

"What? That doesn't make any sense. You just...you know on Friday. Please don't tell me you are one of those men who need it every day!"

"No, I am not a man who needs to make love every day, but there is a big damned difference in you wiggling upside down across the room and me giving myself a happy ending, and actually being inside of you. I am a grown ass man, Jacquetta and half a slice of cake is not going to sate my appetite!"

"Is that what you need - to taste the cake?"

Orlando flung the covers back and got up out of the bed. "I'm going to sleep in the other room tonight," he said as he grabbed his pillow and put it in front of him.

"Oh no you don't! You said we could talk, let's talk," she flung her covers off and stood up. She grabbed her pajama bottoms and pulled them off throwing the pants at him. "What... you want to taste the cake...would that help?"

"Put your damned pants back on and get your ass back in that bed!"

"Will you make up your mind on what you want me to do...I want to kiss you some more. I want you to kiss me, why is this so difficult?" she implored. She put her jammy bottoms back on and climbed in the bed.

"It's difficult because of how much I want you," he said as he sat down on the side of her bed. "Jacquetta, I can't just lick the bowl. I'm going to want to put my finger in the batter then stick the spatula in and fold in the whipped cream. I haven't been sexually active so I am starving. Between work and getting this house ready...that has been my life. I can't simply...I don't have the discipline to be able to walk away from you and not make love to you like you deserve," he confessed.

She was starting to cry and he hated that. He was powerless against her tears. She was sniffling as she spoke in a defeated tone. "All I wanted was a good night kiss," she said through her sniffles.

He snapped at her, "Fine! Fine!"

This was spoken as he came back around the bed and slid inside the covers. He stuck the pillow between their bodies as he leaned over to press his lips against hers. Jacquetta surprised him by running her fingers through his hair, tugging on the tresses until he opened his mouth. The moment he did, her tongue darted inside to mate with his. She gave a little moan into his mouth and a switch clicked on inside of him.

Damn the pillow. He threw it out of the way and pulled her on top of him. His hand slid low to her hips filling his hands with her hocks. Orlando's hands were massaging the flesh as he deepened the kiss with his arms wrapped around her, "You feel so damned good in my arms 'Quetta."

"You feel pretty damn good too husband," she told him as she pushed the covers aside.

He rolled her to her back, his weight on top of her, his hands sliding under the pajama top. The feel of her breast in his hand made him moan loudly. The sound of his guttural vocalization made her bold. She reached low. He was past ready as her hand slipped into his pajama bottoms and took hold of him. He was rock hard and ready. The size of him was vastly different in a ready state than one of rest. He was right, it was a really nice instrument.

An instrument of pleasure.

My instrument for my pleasure. She clamped her hand on him and began to stroke him slowly.

"Shit! Shit! Shit!" he said with a deep throated need as his mouth began to assault hers while he moved in her hand. "Don't stop 'Quetta, please don't stop." His lips trailed down her neck, kissing her throat until he reached her breast. Orlando took one taut bud in his mouth and she cried out.

He knew he couldn't use his fingers but there wasn't a damned thing wrong with his knuckles. His hand slipped inside her pajamas, careful to not place his hands inside of her underwear, as his knuckles ran down the split, she nearly came off the bed. Pressure was applied while the knuckles of his fisted fingers moved up and down bringing her pleasure. She lapsed into French, then into Italian until finally she bucked hard against his hand, digging the nails of her left hand into his back as her right hand squeezed, tugged, and rotated in a circle. His breathing was rapid as his mouth found hers again and he moved, pumping his hips into her hand.

"Whooooo!" he yelled into her mouth and he pumped faster and faster until his right leg began to shake. He lay still atop her, feeling silly because that was all it took - her hand on him and a few tugs. Orlando kissed her softly before he rose slowly from the bed and headed to the bath and started the shower. The jet stream from his modifications to the shower heads started pumping billowing steam, fogging up the bathroom. The soiled clothes were tossed in the hamper as he stepped into the hot water, allowing it to cover his body and rinse away his doubts.

He felt a hand on his back as he turned to find his wife in the shower with him. A large sponge was soaped as she used it to make sudsy circles along his spine.

"Do you realize that this is the first time in almost six years that I have seen you naked?" he said to her.

"But it won't be your last," she told him as she turned him to face her and she pulled him into her arms. "The idea of making love with you is beginning to sit real nice with me. I love you Orlando Flynn."

"I love you as well," he told her. "Everything is going to work out just fine for us."

"I don't have any doubts."

He wished he felt the same way. After wanting her for so long, concerns over his performance when the actual time arose, sat heavily upon his shoulders. If all it took was a couple of tugs on her hand to make him become 15 years old again, what was going to happen when he actually got to make love to her.

Just don't embarrass yourself too much Flynn.

Chapter 15- An Untitled Friendship

The morning was quiet as husband and wife entered the kitchen. Jacquetta's mind was on coffee while Orlando was focused on consuming large quantities of protein. Even in his pajamas, he kept his cell phone close by, something she noticed. What made it odd was that he very seldom received any calls or text messages.

As soon as he poured his first cup of the coffee, his phone buzzed. He slid his finger over the screen putting the call on speaker, "This is Flynn." The sound coming from the phone was a gargle, and it sounded as if someone was hitting the floor.

Orlando looked at Jacquetta and yelled, "On me, 'Quetta!" He made a beeline for the front door, disarming the alarm and running at top speed across the front yard to Guy's house. Orlando didn't even bother to run up the front steps, but did a flying leap over the half dead hedges to land on the porch. He felt above the front door and found the key, turning the knob letting himself into Guy's house. The alarm beeped as he entered the code to disarm the system.

"Guy, I'm here," he yelled as he searched room to room. Jacquetta stayed on his six as he moved through each space, looking, double checking, and searching for their neighbor. They found him upstairs on the bedroom floor, his cell phone inches away from his hand as he twitched and convulsed. "Run downstairs and get me the wooden spoon on the sink," Orlando told her.

Jacquetta's bare feet bounded down the stairs to the

kitchen. The spoon was right on the sink as she grabbed it and ran as fast as she could back up the stairs to the bedroom. Orlando was on the floor, speaking softly to Guy as she handed him the spoon. He forced Guy's mouth open as he used the utensil to keep his neighbor from swallowing his tongue.

"Get his phone please 'Quetta. Hang up the call to me, and scroll through his call history and find the name Marla, give her a call and put it on speaker," Orlando asked.

"Shouldn't I call an ambulance instead?"

"No, this is a small seizure," he told her.

To Jacquetta, it looked like a big one but she didn't argue as she dialed the number. The call was answered on the first ring. "Hey Daddy," a soft voice came over the line.

"Marla, it's me, Orlando," was all he got to say.

"Is my Daddy okay? Is it another seizure? Is it a small one or a grand Mal?" Marla wanted to know.

"It is a small one, but Marla, they are coming more frequently. I just happened to be home this morning," he told her.

Guy had stopped shaking as much and seemed to be coming out of it.

"I will come get him this evening," Marla said.

"Actually, me and Jacquetta are headed your way today, I can bring him and save you the trip," he told her.

Marla wanted to know, "Who is Jacquetta?"

"My wife," he told her.

"What? Shut the front door! You got married. What happened to that fruitcake Becca?"

"We will chat about that when I get there," Orlando said.

"Okay, that's fine. Can you pack Daddy a week's worth of clothing? I am looking at a few facilities here, so I may go ahead and put that house on the market," she said.

Guy had finally stopped seizing. He slurred a bit when he spoke, "I ain't leaving my home to come down there and stay with a bunch of old people who like to play Gin Rummy all damned day."

"I see you are getting back to yourself," Orlando said to the grouchy man.

It suddenly dawned on Guy where he was. His face became stoic when he realized his head was in Orlando's lap. He was frowning as he stared at the floor when he said to him, "You'd better be wearing some pants or something you candied ass weirdo. My head better not be in your lap and your junk is sticking in my ear or some crap!"

Orlando rolled Guy off his lap. He was frowning back at the man, "I thought you would like being close enough to smell my..."

"Orlando!" Jacquetta yelled at him.

"What? He is never going to live this down either way because a Special Forces Army Ranger had to come over here and save his old dirty leather neck!" Orlando said.

"Is that what this is about...this hostility between you? That he is a Marine and you are Army?" she asked.

Both Orlando and Guy looked at her, like two kids put in time out. They were both sitting on the floor with their legs sticking out in front of them. Guy was the first to comment, "What did you think it was about?"

"I thought it was some stupid guy grudge," she told them both.

"No, we are friends. We grew up together. Guy is a few years older but this cantankerous nut buster has been a friend of Woodson's for years. He basically grew up in the house with us," he told her.

"So all of this name calling..." she mumbled.

"He is still an ignorant fart bag," Orlando said.

Guy was crawling up to his knees to get in a standing position. "And he is still a runny Hershey squirt, but we take care of each other. I like having you take care of me too Ms. 'Quetta," Guy said this as he wiggled his eyebrows at her.

"Shut up you old puss bucket. Get packed, we are taking you to Marla's. We leave in an hour or so," Orlando told him.

He left Guy sitting on the side of the bed as he handed him back his phone. "You were lucky I was home this time," he told him.

"Yeah, I guess I am going to have to give 'Quetta my number," he waggled his brows again.

"No, we are going to put our heads together with Marla and create a new plan. Once we begin having children, she is not going to be able to come over her and climb these stairs and help you during a seizure. Something has to be done Guy," he said with no emotion in his voice.

"I know. I am trying to get there," Guy said.

It did not take the three of them long to get loaded up in the truck. "I have to stop by the bank first Orlando," she told him.

"Is everything okay?"

"Yeah, I just need to pick up something from Courtney," she told him.

True to her word, she ran in the bank and came out by the time he had found a parking space. The ride to Valdosta was uneventful as Guy slept in the back seat.

"I want to talk to you about last night," she said to him in a whisper.

Orlando looked in the back seat at Guy pretending to be asleep. "There is nothing to discuss," he told her as he exited the interstate and pulled up to a small office building. A pretty young woman in her early twenties came out to greet them.

Her dark wavy hair caught a gust of wind and blew into her face. Guy was watching her out the window. "I swear she looks more and more like Maria every day."

"Your daughter is lovely," Jacquetta told him as she helped him out of the vehicle. It was hard to imagine that Guy was close in age to Woodson. He was the saddest looking 44 year-old she had seen in all of her life. He looked more like he was 76 and ready to die.

She greeted Marla with a smile, "I am Jacquetta, Orlando's wife."

Marla stood there gawking at her, not sure what to say. "I know, people are surprised to find that I have long hair," Jacquetta said to the young woman.

A young woman with no filters. "Long hair? Heck, I had no idea that Orlando was down with the swirl. You know, especially with Becca being so blond. She was a loon though. Her ways of thinking are bass ackwards and country as hell. The logic that she comes up with is something to be reckoned with…. You know it would not surprise me a bit if she was making up some wild tale so she could push him to do something she wanted, and it backfired on her nutty ass."

Jacquetta was now gawking at her.

"I know, I know. I just hit you with a beehive full of information and you are looking at me like I have lost my mind. Seriously though, wait until you meet her. You'll see what I mean. She is nucking futz!" Marla told her.

Without a blink of her eye, she turned to her father, "Come over here old man. I think you make yourself have these seizures so you can come down here and be with me.

Guy gave her a feeble smile. "I don't want to be a nuisance Marla, you have your own life. You don't need to be worried about me."

"I'm gonna worry Daddy. You are not well and we will have to make some decisions here real soon. This is not going to go on," Marla told him as she waved goodbye to Orlando. "It was nice meeting you Jacquetta. I will be up this weekend for the cookout, and I hope to spend some time with you."

"That would be lovely," Jacquetta told her. She climbed into the truck and looked at her husband. "What is wrong with Guy?"

"He's dying. And if you ask me, he is taking the long way around," Orlando said.

"Is there a shortcut you would prefer him to take?" she

wanted to know.

"No, there's not but he won't take his meds, he misses half of his appointments, he still smokes, won't use his oxygen tank and he eats like crap. Half of his medical issues are because he smokes and eats like crap," Orlando said as he drove towards the dealership.

"Well, do you think it would help if I took him a plate every now and then?" she asked him.

"Hell no! He is like a stray dog, if you start feeding him, he never goes away!"

"But you said he eats poorly..."

"He eats that way because he wants to, not because he can't take care of himself. Guy was a cook in the Marines. For a while he had a little bistro over by the campus, but his health took a turn for the worse, and now he is on disability. He sits at home all day watching Netflix and porn," Orlando said.

"Did you notice how his right arm has that Popeye effect?" Orlando simulated a hand movement with an up and down motion like he was shaking a set a dice.

"It does not!" She started to laugh.

He turned his head to look at his wife. "...And you! Stay out from over there. If he makes a move, you kick his ass defending yourself and you may kill him."

Jacquetta could not believe what Orlando was saying. There was a lull in the conversation as she looked for the right time to change the subject. He didn't want to discuss last night, but she also had to handle what was coming up in front of them.

"Uhmm, Orlando. I don't want a used car. I have been saving up, and I have the money to get me a new car, that's why I went to the bank."

He pulled into the Ford dealership to be greeted by a friend of Orlando's from high school, Tommy Tutwiler. All the kids back then called him tee-tee because of his initials and he wet the bed all the way into the tenth grade. Old habits die hard. Orlando waved at the man. "What's up Tee-Tee?"

Tommy was not amused. "You are an asshole Orlando Flynn! How you got lucky enough to win this beautiful woman is beyond me. Hey there 'Quetta!"

The shock on Orlando's face was comical. "How the hell you know my wife Tee-Tee?"

"I was in the bank when she came in on Saturday," he told Orlando. Tommy turned his attention to Jacquetta. "I have your car all ready, washed, waxed and fueled up. We only need the check and your signature and you are ready to go!"

"Thank you Tommy," she told him as she handed him the envelope. "I can't wait to drive my new baby!"

Orlando didn't like surprises. This was a surprise to him. He loved that his wife was independent, but he wanted to get her a car. He had planned to get her a new one next year, but she had enough to buy a brand new car without his help. He was starting to think there were some things about his wife that he had yet to learn. Being able to dance like a professional stripper was one thing, but the money to buy a new car straight out...was another. A fear washed over him.

Oh no, she had been paying her bills by being a stripper.

Chapter 16 – Say What Now?

"You thought I was a what?" Jacquetta belted out loud. In the quiet of their home, she looked at her husband over meatloaf and mashed potatoes like he had lost his relationship with Jesus.

"I mean it is okay. It is your past, there is no shame in doing that to make ends meet," he told her as he stared into his pile of potatoes.

"Orlando, seriously? I was a gymnast until my parents were killed in that accident. After, they died, I went to live with my grandparents and they couldn't drive me to all the matches. My coach wanted me to stay with her, but Grandma had just lost her only daughter and I was all she had left, so I moved to Kennesaw. I stopped gymnastics, but I still loved to dance. A few years ago, I took some pole dancing classes for fitness, and combine that with my gymnastic ability, I can move...," she told him.

Several looks crossed his face but the obvious one was a look of relief. "I have to ask, though, paying cash for a car, 'Quetta?"

"Orlando, I am not broke, you just assumed that I was," she told him with a smile. "Go on, eat up before your dinner gets cold."

The evening ended quietly with him giving her curious glances as he watched his favorite Monday night show. To her surprise, he was still fully clothed most of the day. Before heading to bed, she asked for his help moving the guest bed so she could paint the wall.

"Since you asked me a question, I want to ask you one," she said.

"Shoot! I am an open naked book," he said with a grunt as he moved the heavy bed.

"Yeah...about that, why are you always naked?"

Orlando laughed a bit. "It started innocently enough. I liked the feel of not having the weight of clothes on me. You know, clothes have a certain placement in your life in the spectrum of the universe."

"Say what now?" she asked with a laugh. "Break that down a bit for me."

He sat on the side of the bed, one knee bent. "I am the youngest of three boys. When I understood that no one wants to wrestle with you, give you wet Willie's or sit on you to hold you down, if you are naked- it changed my young life. After that, it was easy. If I put the remote in my lap, neither Woodson nor Christopher would try to take it, so I got to watch whatever I wanted. No one bothered me," he told her.

"You are a grown man now, but you are still naked most of the time," she inquired.

"We went to Catholic School, so we wore uniforms. I worked in the store on weekends, and I wore a Flynn Hardware shirt," he said. Orlando pulled at the shirt he had on which read Flynn Hardware.

"I played sports, I wore a uniform. I joined the Army, I wore a uniform. In my home, I am me. I don't belong to anyone but you. Besides, it really limits unwanted guests and cousins hanging around my house drinking up my beer and eating up my food," he said.

"I'm tired, I am headed to bed. You coming?" He was done with the conversation as he headed toward the bathroom to ready himself for bed.

"Be there in a sec, I need to tidy up a bit," she told him.

Tuesday morning sped by as Jacquetta painted the wall behind the bed in the guest room. Once the mint green paint dried, she knew a few irises on the wall in purple would make the room pop. With her favorite brushes in hand, what began as a few large flowers turned into a whole field of irises that would rival Van Gogh's painting.

The feel of the brushes in her hand was almost magical as she moved to the water closet in the hall and quickly painted two children at a lakeside chasing ducks. Jacquetta stepped back to admire the handy work. "Oh!" she exclaimed as she remembered the duckling rugs and matching bath ware.

"I love it!" she said as she looked at her watch. It was four o'clock and she had missed lunch. It only took 30 minutes to clean her brushes, shower and put on some fresh clothes before starting dinner. Last night's supper was heavy, so tonight it was going to be a lighter fare of maybe some sautéed chicken breasts, with some grilled romaine leaves and asparagus. Half a grapefruit was left over from breakfast along with some grapes and cheese from the weekend.

At a quarter of six, the doorbell rang. Jacquetta went to the door to find Maggie Mae on the doorstep. "Hey there,

Ms. Maggie, come on in. I am setting up for dinner, but I can put on some coffee, if you like."

Maggie stepped inside the house and noticed the paintings on the wall. Her eyes were wide. "I smell fresh paint, and the chicken smells wonderful," she said.

"I was doing some painting today," she smiled at her mother-in-law. "Come on, I'll show you," she said as she led the lady to the hall water closet.

Maggie Mae peered in the bathroom and her mouth was wide. As Jacquetta led her down the hall to the guest room, she showed off her handy work on the wall of irises. "I am torn between putting the bed back there or allowing the wall to breathe and fill the room with the life of the flowers," Jacquetta said.

Suddenly, Maggie Mae pulled Jacquetta into her arms. Her cheeks staining with tears. "I was so worried about him, but you are perfect. Just what he needs."

Jacquetta hugged her back as she heard the familiar jangle of her husband's keys when he came in through the back door.

"Come on Ms. Maggie, I promised you a cup of coffee and I have some pie left over from last night," she said as she pulled her mother-in-law by the hand down the hall.

A quick kiss was given to her handsome breadwinner after he hugged his mother, then disappeared down the hallway and Jacquetta started the coffee. It did not take long before Orlando came back down the hall, wearing only those damned house slippers.

"How was your day Ma?"

"It was good Sweetie, and yours?"

"Same ole same ole. You staying for dinner? Dad playing poker tonight?"

"No, I just came to see if Jacquetta needed help with anything," Maggie Mae answered.

It was a surreal moment for Jacquetta as she watched the interaction with her very naked husband and his mother. "It doesn't bother you that your grown son is only wearing a pair of slippers?"

Orlando yelled from the comfort of his chair, "She has seen this with and without hair. She don't care!"

Maggie Mae sipped on her freshly poured cup of coffee, mouthing *I don't*. "We had him tested when he was a kid to make sure he was normal. And that joker tested at nearly genius level!"

"Did you hear that 'Quetta, we are going to have genius babies!" He called to her from his Big Daddy chair in the den.

She only hoped their genius babies would enjoy wearing clothes. Because the more she saw him naked, the thirstier she was becoming. Orlando was looking like a very cold bottle of water on a hot July day.

Chapter 17 - Butchered

Wednesday morning was the first opportunity to head into the back yard to take a good look at her studio. She opened the doors as the sun shone through giving her perfect morning light. Suddenly, she felt inspired and grabbed a blank canvas, a few brushes and set to work. Small town Americana wasn't really her area, but the idea of the hardware store on Main Street with Harlan standing on the porch by the cigar Indian with a cup of coffee in his hand gave her a warm feeling.

Time got away from her and she looked at her watch, it was almost five. She did a mental assessment of leftovers and there wasn't enough of any one thing to make a meal. A cup of soup and sandwich would have sufficed for her, but Orlando liked meat. In her haste to get to her shop, she had completely forgotten to take something out for dinner.

"Crap," she mumbled as she stuck her brushes in water and closed up the studio. She grabbed her car keys off the peg in the kitchen along with her clutch purse and drove over to the butcher's shop.

Mr. Baldwin acted as if she were a movie star. "Hey there 'Quetta! I have the ribs on sale for this weekend's cookout. What are you and Orlando planning to throw on the grill?"

Truth was, she had no idea. "I guess, give me a couple of rib eyes, and I need something easy to cook tonight."

"Let's see, you want some pork chops? I have three of those left. I have a veal shank, but that is a slow simmer, and I have a rib roast," Mr. Baldwin said.

"The veal and rib roast will take too long, I will take the chops," she answered as the doorbell jangled. In walked none other than her father-in-law.

Jacquetta gave him a bright smile. "Hi Dad! I was just grabbing a couple of steaks for the cookout on Saturday. I also was trying to figure out what to cook tonight for dinner. Orlando is such a carnivore."

She was still wearing her painting smock, and to her surprise, Harlan didn't jump this time when she called him Dad. Instead he surprised her when he said, "Yeah, he gets that from me. I am cutting back on some of it, trying to take off a few pounds, but you know how those things go."

"Do I ever..." she said with a great deal of understanding in her voice. She paid for her meats and thanked Mr. Baldwin.

"Dad," she called before exiting the door.

"Yeah?" he said.

"The front door is always open. I keep a fresh pot of coffee on, a nice dessert and good conversation anytime you want it," she told him.

"That means a lot Jacquetta. Thank you," Harlan told her.

Mr. Baldwin wasted no time focusing his attention on Harlan Flynn. "Your son is one lucky cuss snagging that one! Guy came in here to get some lamb chops and he could not stop bragging about the ones she had cooked and brought over to him for dinner. That cake she cooked on Sunday was like a slice of heaven in your mouth, and I hear that son of yours is wearing clothes around the house. Ms.

Marvin said she can open her kitchen curtains again!"

Harlan only stood watching the man. Jake Baldwin was a great butcher, but he was also the biggest gossip in town, but it was heartwarming to know that what he was spreading was good news about his son for a change.

"Yeah Jake, my Maggie Mae dropped in on her yesterday and said she had painted the house real nice, and had her art up on the wall and everything. I want to see some of those pictures she paints. I may buy one for the house," Harlan said with pride.

"Oh yeah, do you think she would sell me one for my anniversary...I wanted to get something different for my Rose this year. We are celebrating 45 years of marriage," Mr. Baldwin said.

"That's real good. I will ask Jacquetta if she has some for sale," Harlan told him as he placed his order for Saturday's cookout.

The cookout was right around the corner. Harlan had been worried when Jake told him that Becca was returning home this weekend. Initially he was convinced that the marriage of his son to the black woman was a ruse to get the community from seeing him as a chump. It didn't seem like that anymore. Jacquetta was a lovely woman and she was growing on him a lot. Maggie Mae's visit yesterday only solidified his wishes that his odd son would find the right woman.

By all accounts, it seemed like Orlando had.

Chapter 18 – An Untitled Love

It started off as a really odd day. An unsettled feeling washed over Jacquetta as she went about her daily routines. She finally managed to get most of the boxes unpacked and all of the china placed in the cabinet. Her energy level was a little low today as she put a chicken in a roasting pan to slow cook for dinner. They could eat off that bird for a day or two, which would save her from cooking tomorrow.

A cup of coffee in hand, she started from the front of the house and walked all the way through to the back looking, checking and making certain everything was complete and pleasing to the eye.

A few plants here and there and it will be perfect.

The timer was set on the oven as she grabbed a magazine and took a seat.

Home.

I have a home.

Dark memories of not belonging anywhere filled her head after the death of her parents. Although her grandparents loved her, she never felt as if their home was her home. She had joined the Army right after college to get a chance to travel a bit on the government's dime and her assignment at NATO was perfect. Italy was everything she had hoped it would be as she perfected her art studies.

The assignment in Kandahar was a fluke. She wasn't supposed to be there but it was a cancellation on someone else's part that opened the door for Jacquetta to be shoved through. A random dose of sickness and her life had been altered. For the first time in six years, she was no longer looking at the whole incident as something horrible that happened to her. Today, Jacquetta was seeing the incident as something horrible that happened to her that could have been a whole lot worse if it had not been for Orlando Flynn.

My husband.

Orlando Flynn is my husband.

Tonight, she planned to become his wife in every sense of the word and give a name to the untitled love they shared. The past was the past, and she was ready get beyond it and start living the life she had imagined. Next week, she would head over to the campus and apply for an adjunct teaching position in the art department. It was also on her list to send cards to all of her friends and family with her new address and name.

"I guess I can finally let them know all of those wedding gifts came in handy," she said as she took the chicken from the stove.

The rice was added to the steamer as she made her way to the bath to grab a quick shower before Orlando got home.

Orlando arrived at 6:15 angrier than a bear with his head stuck in a honey comb. He was so mad, he didn't even bother to undress before he sat in his favorite chair, his head in his hands.

"What's wrong?"

"A tough day. My dad…he is all over the place and in my way. He is giving conflicting orders to employees which is causing a riff in the staff. I didn't want to keep any of the people he had hired because I knew they would still be loyal to him, but firing good workers for no cause is stupid. He is supposed to be retired!"

Orlando had started to scratch his neck. Jacquetta opened a beer and handed him one. "When was the last time your parents took a vacation?"

"My parents think that a vacation is a three day weekend at the lake," he said as he took a sip from his beer. "Thank you, I could have gotten this myself."

"I am your life partner, Orlando. I am here to make things easier for you," she told him.

His eyes came up slowly to eye her breasts, her lips and then meet her eyes. "Thoughtful...of you," he mumbled.

"The money you were going to use for the down payment on the car for me, we can use it to send them on a vacation," she told him.

"You would be okay with that? I mean, I was going to put down four maybe five grand on you a car," he told her.

"Sure, use it on them for an extended vacation," she said. "Do they like to do long drives?"

"I don't know how long, they are older. What do you have in mind?"

She smiled at him as she sat closer on the couch. "When my grandfather retired, or claimed he had retired, and my mother took over the business, he was everywhere and all in her way. My dad bought my grandparents two one-way tickets to Seattle. He rented them a car on that end and handed them a map. Daddy even went as far as booking hotels for them along the way back, building in stops to US landmarks. They saw the Grand Canyon, spent the night in Vegas, I even think they stopped at the Kentucky Derby. They talked about that trip for years. Even after my parent's death, they would have quiet moments when they would talk about little dives they ate in and the like."

She watched his face closely while she spoke to him. "I could map out something like that for your parents, book the hotel rooms, and have them a flight ready to go in two weeks. We can present it to them Saturday at the cookout as a retirement gift. The shop would be yours to rearrange and overhaul while they are gone for a month. It could use some fresh coats of paint..." she told him. "I was even thinking about painting a mural on one of the walls of maybe you and your brothers younger, with your dad, if you could find me the right picture."

Orlando said nothing as she watched her. His chest constricting in tightness from her words. Emotions which had been locked away were slowly opening as he stared at his lovely wife.

His silence was a bit unnerving to Jacquetta. She asked, "I think that would help a lot don't you Orlando?"

A crackly voice responded to her, "That would be great 'Quetta. You sure? I mean taking five grand from our household to blow on my parents..."

"They deserve it and you deserve it as well. If your plans for Flynn Hardware don't coincide with Harlan's, he needs to be given something else to focus on," she told him.

The tension had left his face.

"Is there any other issue I can help you solve today husband?" she asked with a coy smile.

"MMMhmmm," he said as he looked at her, his gaze full of passion. "I still need to burn off some of this tension."

"I will get my sneaks if you want to go for a run," she answered him with a blank stare knowing what he needed from her.

"I don't want to run 'Quetta. I want to be with my wife. I require some time with my wife," he said flatly.

"Okay," she told him.

His eyebrows shot up. "Okay what?"

"Let's spend some time."

His lips were tight. "I am not talking about playing a hand of Pinochle."

"I know what you are talking about. I said okay," she told him.

"Don't play with me 'Quetta. I am tense. I am frustrated and sleeping next to your sexy little tight body every night is keeping me horny as hell. I don't want a tug and a kiss either, or a fancy lap dance... I *need* my wife," he said.

She stood up and reached for his hand. "Dinner will be cold, but if you need me right now, then let's go."

Orlando sat for a minute looking at her trying to gauge if she was sincere.

"Seriously?" He asked her.

Her answer was to start walking towards the bedroom. Orlando was on his feet with her in his arms as he carried her down the hall and deposited her none to gently on the bed. He closed the door and reached for her pants. Jacquetta had no time to react as he flipped her to her stomach, tugging her pants over her hips. Orlando dropped to the floor behind her and buried his face.

It felt so marvelous that she crawled to her knees with her butt poking in the air as she balled the bed covers into her fingers while she bit into the pillow. "Damn!" she yelled as his tongue swirled in her sweet spot. How he managed to get undressed as he warmed her up was beyond her.

In a gentle motion he shimmied her pants over her thighs, and off her legs as he flipped her over to her back.

Jacquetta tried to sit up, but his hand pushed her back onto the bed. "Orlando, do you want me to return..."

His voice was gruff when he answered, "I'm past that point." He reached for her blouse but didn't bother with the buttons as he yanked the top open, pushed her bra above her breasts exposing the mounds to the cool air of the room. The buds hardened as the chillness from the air conditioned space forced the capillaries to contract. Orlando took the mounds into his hands, massaging the orbs before slurping a bud into his mouth like a string of spaghetti then suckling at her like a babe. Wondrous sensations were shooting through her body as the feel of him atop her made her moan aloud, nearly cooing as the jolts of pleasure ricocheted through her senses.

"Uhmm, I like that sound 'Quetta," he said as he suckled at her other breast, getting the same response.

"Kiss me, Orlando," she moaned.

His mouth found hers as he positioned his desire and kissed her deeply, pressing himself into her in an attempt to connect their bodies. For Jacquetta, it had been so long, her body could not accommodate his initial try. Her breath lodged in her throat as the tip of his intentions pressed greedily forward. Orlando froze as the tightness of his wife surrounded the tip of him, his body relishing the feel of finally connecting with her. She needed time to adjust to his attempts, but for him, too much time had passed and he desired to be all the way inside of her. He wanted her as his wife in every way. He loved her more now than he ever had before, as she patiently attempted to accommodate the surprising size of him in ready mode. If it killed him, or broke him down, he was going to make it good for her, but his need was taking over his common sense. Slowly he began to move inside of her. Sweat built on his forehead as he worked to bring her as much pleasure as he could, trying desperately to stave off an abrupt ending.

His held her close as his hips rocked in incremental movements, drilling into her, asking her body to accept his entry. Orlando maintained a steady rhythm, stroking her internally with an even sway of his hips, each movement penetrating deeper. His mouth stayed attached to hers, his tongue mating with hers as he did the same with their bodies. The depth of his penetration increased as he felt her begin to relax to take him all in. Jacquetta slowly began to move with him which almost caused his undoing.

"You feel so good inside of me," she moaned into the side of his neck. She raised her knees towards her chest, bringing them up along his sides, sucking him deeper into her love. Orlando groaned loudly. He needed to move. He need to get deeper.

"On me 'Quetta," he commanded. She knew the three word instruction all too well. It meant when he moved, she moved with him. There was no thought involved. If he went left, she would follow. If he went right, she would follow.

Orlando's fingers dug into the fleshy parts of her hips as he picked up his pace. She, with a handful of his hair, moved in unison with him. Each stroke he pushed down, she brought her hips up. Suddenly, he broke the connection, pulling away from her, disconnecting the wonderful vibrations he was building deep inside of her as his mouth went back to her sweet spot.

"You taste so good," he told her as his tongue swirled, teased and brought her to the precipice of explosion.

He raised her right leg high onto his shoulder as he came face to face with her again and thrust back into her, pushing her, encouraging, demanding her to let go.

"Orlando," she panted his name as her pleasure began to build.

"Stay with me baby," he told her as he increased his pace again. His hips moved, creating a rhythm that was magical as the sensations built from her midsection downward and she let go, crying out his name as she clung to him.

"That's it, 'Quetta. That's it baby," he whispered. His mouth was open as he panted like a large wet dog trying to catch his breath. She felt so good, he could barely hold on another second. "You feel so amazing," he praised her when he began his finish with long, deep, penetrating thrusts. Orlando needed this release. He needed the connection. He needed his 'Quetta. He lowered his head and kissed her hard, his tongue snaking inside her mouth as his body smushed hers underneath his weight, while his hips bored even deeper as he reached his own climax. Orlando called her name as husky grunts crept up from the base of his throat into her ear.

In his mind he was telling his wife how beautiful she was. In his mind he told her how wonderful it had been to make love with her. In his mind, he had given her the best three minutes of her life. He lay still, holding her close afterwards, speaking to her softly.

"I'm sorry, that wasn't very romantic," he said. "It didn't last very long either."

"It was exactly what we both needed."

"You needed your husband to be a great deal more gentle and understanding," he told her. His throat was raspy when he said, "I apologize, but I was thirsty as hell."

"I was coming up on a bad case of cotton mouth myself," she told him as she planted small kisses on his shoulder, neck and face.

"You know 'Quetta, that was good as hell," he said with a chuckle as he pulled her into his arms. "Now I am hungry."

Her fingers trailed over the fine hairs of his abdomen. "Yeah, that was pretty intense. The chicken is cold but that loving was not!"

Slowly, they made their way back to the kitchen, sitting at the table, snacking on cold chicken and mushy rice. The evening was quiet as husband and wife shared intimate glances laced with promises of how much better it would be the next time they made love.

"So...," Jacquetta said as she spooned in a mouthful of rice. "...That's what I have been missing all these years?"

The look on his face was soft and filled with love, "It's okay, it gives me a reason to play catch up."

Jacquetta was all warm on the inside and anxious to get back to the bedroom; she wanted to play some more. Somewhere in the middle of the night, after the dinner had settled, he made love to his wife again. This time with no fervent need for a release, but a desire for intimacy and connection. He spoke lovingly to her as he brought her pleasure and explored every inch of her body. They had crossed a major obstacle.

There were only a few other hurdles. The first was his parents. The second was the matter of Becca.

Becca would be home tomorrow.

Chapter 19- Slow and Easy

To Jacquetta's surprise, Harlan stopped by the house on Friday morning. She handed him a cup of coffee as he took his time walking through the house, admiring her paintings as if he were in the Metropolitan Museum of Art. It was an odd feeling watching her father-in-law as he stood in the guest bedroom staring at the irises on the wall.

"It is almost as if I am standing in the field in the midst of the flowers. This is amazing Jacquetta. You are very talented," he told her.

His eyes were watery when he turned to face her. "I wanted to travel a great deal, but you know, I inherited the store when I was 24 years old. I got married to Maggie Mae and then Woodson came along, and before I knew it... well, you know."

"I don't know Mr. Flynn, please tell me more," she encouraged him.

He was smiling when he raised his eyes to her. "There is nothing to tell. I did what I needed to do for my wife and my boys. I am just happy that Orlando found the right woman."

The cup which held his coffee, he washed and placed in the drain as he nodded his head to her, "See you tomorrow, Jacquetta. Thanks for the coffee and allowing me to visit. You have a lovely and warm home."

"Again, the door is always open," she told him.

As he stood in the doorway, he looked back at the painting on the living room wall. "I would like to buy one of those paintings from you, if possible. I know Jake Baldwin said he wanted one. Is that doable?"

"For you, anything is doable," she told him.

This answered satisfied him as he walked out the door. At some point she was going to have to tell her husband she wasn't well known in America, but in Europe her paintings went for a pretty penny. Jacquetta had been playing with the idea of presenting a few paintings to her new family for Christmas. *Maybe, if I get started now...*

Jacquetta couldn't wait for her husband to come home from work. She played it cool with him even though she had been hot all day. The man stuck out his tongue to lick his lips and she had to cross her legs. It didn't really help her condition much as Orlando kept giving her sexy looks throughout dinner. He watched her as if he were remembering every movement they made together last night. Jacquetta couldn't lie; several times during the day she had been tempted to make a booty call to the hardware store and give him a new kind of lunch on that great big desk in his office. Initiating sex had never been her thing but she felt flirty.

"You keep looking at me like you want some of this," she told him. She leaned forward with her breasts resting on the table.

"I keep looking at you like I am going to get some of that," he said as he pushed the liver and onions around on his plate.

"I take it you are not a fan of liver," she stated.

"I like it just fine. I just don't want onion breath later when I am kissing you goodnight," he winked at her.

Jacquetta went from being flirty to feeling bold. "It only matters to the set of lips you plan to kiss."

Orlando started to choke. "I do declare Mrs. Flynn that kind of talk is making a soldier blush."

She stood and walked around the small kitchen table coming up beside him. Her arms slipped around his neck as she whispered in his ear several other things that made his cheeks pink up, his pants get tight, and his pupils dilate. "Damn," was all he said as he pulled her onto his lap.

"I have not been able to concentrate all day. All I could think about was getting home to you," he spoke softly.

"I had more I wanted to tell you Orlando," she told him as she reached for his shirt. She pulled hard, yanking it out of the waistband of his pants, trying to pull it over his head. The rest of what she wanted to tell him was lost as his mouth covered hers in a passionate kiss.

"Don't tell...show me," he said as he stood slowly, his wife in his arms. Orlando was in no hurry as he carried her down the hall to their bedroom. He sat on the bed, her small frame still in his arms, slowly leaning back into the firmness of the mattress. His body was ready for her, as her hands moved low to rub him. Small moans escaped his lips as she unzipped his pants, freeing him, touching her man, making him feel loved. She moved quickly, getting him out of his pants. Jacquetta was anxious as she struggled to get out her clothing, urging him out his own.

Orlando put his hand on her abdomen, pushing her flat

onto the bed. "I've hungered to be with you all day, and I have no plans to rush my way through it," he stated as his body covered hers. He kissed her slow, his tongue exploring her mouth, his fingers exploring her body. Jacquetta moved impatiently against him, but it didn't matter to Orlando. He was in the mood to take it real slow and easy.

Chapter 20 - Unacknowledged

It was a hot Saturday and the sun beamed down on Milligan's Park as Woodson Flynn arrived in the dually Ford F450 pulling the Flynn Holiday Grill. It was a massive charcoal burning grill that was 8 feet from end to end and six feet across. It was an uncovered grilled that could be accessed from either side once the fire and coals were hot.

The men loaded in cut up pieces of hickory wood, charcoal and chicory chunks allowing the pieces to marinate in lighter fluid before setting it all aflame. Roman Carter, the local barber, came along with a gas can and doused the wood incensing all the men folks.

"Dang it Roman, it's gonna burn too hot and need more wood. Stay your butt over there with the cooler!" Harlan yelled at his longtime friend.

"I was only trying to help get it going. Families are going to be arriving soon and we don't even have the fires hot enough to roast a wiener," Roman snapped back.

"The only wiener we are going to be roasting is you Roman, you knuckle headed frankfurter," Jake called out from the mound of tent poles he was fighting to assemble. "Someone get over here and help with this dang fool tent."

Thirty minutes later, the beer tent was assembled, the tables were set, the grill was going and the first of Venture's residents began to show up for the annual Fourth of July picnic. It was almost noon when Orlando and Jacquetta arrived. The Flynn family tent was set up near the far corner of the grille.

Jacquetta had brought along her Grandma Edith's favorite quilt. The bright colors of the fabric pieces is what made Jacquetta want to paint. The way her Grandmother laid in the scraps of fabric replicated a Renoir that she later saw on display at a museum in Verona. She thought it was perfect for today's festivities.

Orlando looked sharp in a pair of khaki shorts and a Flynn Hardware red polo shirt. Since it was going to be such a hot, sticky and long day, she opted for a pair of white pedal pushers and a soft pink tee. The moment she spread out the quilt under the tent, people began to flock over to greet the town's newest resident and the wife of Orlando Flynn. Many had heard about her, others gossiped about her, while several just wanted to glance at the black woman Orlando had brought home to Venture.

The DJ, who happened to be Rodney, had set up in his tent, the dance floor was laid out and the water slide was started. Kids arrived with frazzled Moms who carried coolers, pushed strollers and found spots in the grass to set up camp for the day's activities. The fireworks would start after dark but in the meantime, a game of cards were underway under the main Gazebo. The smaller gazebo had a few men playing a game of dominoes while others told fishing stories of the one that got away.

Becca should have waited under that gazebo to start her tale about the one that got away. She arrived a few minutes after 3 pm. Jacquetta knew it was Becca because every eye in the park seemed to turn to her. She kept her eyes down on the magazine she'd brought and ignored the stares. The pronounced belly led the way to the Flynn family tent as the dark haired Frenchman walked alongside her.

Becca made a beeline for the Flynn tent. Orlando was not in it, but at the grill, which caused the pretty blond to turn and head in that direction instead. A light tap was made on Orlando's shoulder as he turned to spot the woman who had dumped him. He was all smiles as he greeted her. He even touched her belly and shook the Frenchman's hand.

"Orlando, may I have a word alone?" Becca asked him.

"Why? We have no secrets, Becca," he told her. To her companion he added, "Jean Marc, I didn't get your last name." Adding "…All we have is soda and beer, no wine; is a cold beer okay for you?" Orlando asked the Frenchman.

"A beer will work well," Jean Marc answered. "The surname is Beauvais," he spoke again. The French accent was thick.

"Hey Dad, throw me a beer for Becca's new beau," Orlando called out.

Jean Marc watched him with some uncertainty as he accepted the cold drink. It befuddled Becca as well, that her former fiancé was not upset with her. So many people were watching the interaction that no one paid attention to Jacquetta leaving out of the back of the tent and heading over to the DJ booth. She slipped Rodney the thumb drive which contained her husband's favorite playlist. In truth, there was only one song on the list that mattered.

"Rodney, cue up song number one next, please" she asked the man. Right on cue, by the time she made it to the corner of the dance floor *For the Love of You* by the Isley Brothers began to play. This was her husband's favorite song. It didn't matter what he was doing, or who he was doing it with, he would drop whatever he was working on to dance to the music and sing along.

Becca was trying hard to get his undivided attention. Orlando's head snapped left and right as he yelled above the roar of the children going down the water slides. The call for his wife could be heard over the bellows of moms shouting for kids and the fabricated lies of men trying to outdo each other under the gazebo with tales of grandeur.

"Hey 'Quetta, they're playing my jam!" He called out, "Get over here baby, and let's do this!"

It tickled her to no end because her husband had one dance move. The move closely resembled a rich man pulling coins from the fifth pocket of his fancy pants and passing it to the little people in the street – one coin at a time. Orlando often bragged that he had so mastered this move, he could do it high, he could do it low, it could be done fast and it could be done slow.

"Come on "Quetta!" Orlando called again.

She shimmied her shoulders as she moved out on the dance floor and replicated his signature move, while he sang the song out loud and off key. Jacquetta turned her back to him as he moved in close, his hands on her hips. Anyone watching knew the way Orlando moved with his wife, that the couple was in love. There was also something else that was evident to anyone looking – there was a very deep connection between the husband and wife. Becca saw it too.

"Who is that woman?" She asked out loud.

Maggie Mae Flynn had somehow managed to be at Becca's side. She was all too happy to answer the question. "Oh that is Jacquetta. Orlando's wife."

The color drained from her face as her hands gripped her belly and she took a seat.

Orlando had moved on.

This also meant that nothing she had planned was going to work in her favor. Her fiancé had married another woman. A little something her mother had failed to tell her before she boarded the plane home.

Chapter 21 - Whatchamacallit

The park was loaded with families, friends and loved ones. Many friends of Orlando's came over to pat him on the back, others had snarky comments to make about his singing or dancing, or both. To Jacquetta it was a heartwarming scene. Several of the women came over to chat with her about her lemon love cake recipe. One lady even asked her about painting a family portrait. A few surprises came her way that afternoon. The first came from one Hedley Noitan, Dean of the Humanities department at the local college.

"Jacquetta Flynn, I hear you are a painter with an advanced degree in art history," he started the conversation.

"Yes, that is true," she responded.

"You have any time or experience on the podium?" Hedley wanted to know.

"I taught classes at Kennesaw State as an adjunct. I also taught Art History courses in Naples and also in Paris," she told him.

"Great you're hired!" Hedley handed her a business card. "Send me your CV on Monday, schedule an appointment with me to give you a tour of the campus, the art department and the like. There are two sections you will be teaching, a morning and an evening class. The evening class is mixed with grad and undergrad," he told her as he shook her hand.

"Look forward to seeing you on campus," he told Jacquetta. As if nothing had occurred, he walked over to join a group of stodgy looking middle-aged men.

Did he just give me a job?

Her face was twisted as she looked at all the meat on the grill. The sight of all the juicy bratwursts, hot dogs and burgers made her mouth water and tummy rumble. Harlan was manning the grill, or rather half keeping an eye on the flame as he shared fishing stories with a group of his friends. The Devil was sitting on her shoulder whispering in her ear to walk into the center of the men and plant a juicy kiss on Harlan's cheek and call him Dad. Common sense prevailed as she opted instead to walk up quietly and get a burger from the grill.

"Excuse me Mr. Flynn, are any of these burgers and dogs ours?" she asked him.

Harlan's eyebrows shot up. "Oh, it's Mr. Flynn today? Any other time it's Dad!"

This drew the attention of all of his friends who pelted him with questions on the young black woman's identity. How they could not know was beyond her. Everything in the small town spread like wildfire. Among the group of men were none that she recognized with the exception of the Mayor Galley, whose face was plastered on every fifth billboard in the small town.

"Gentlemen," Harlan said, as he leaned back to fill his lungs with air. "This beautiful young lady is my daughter-in-law, Jacquetta. She is an artist. Her work is amazing. " This was her second surprise.

Mayor Galley spoke first, "You don't say. That Christopher finally settled down...good for him."

Harlan was shaking his head. "No. Jacquetta is married

to my youngest, Orlando."

The air seemed to leave the group. The Mayor spoke up first, "You mean to tell me somebody finally married that naked weirdo?"

This was the wrong thing to say because Harlan took offense and went into a boxer's stance with his fists balled up. "I have told you on more than one occasion, you fat bellied blow hard about calling my boy a weirdo! He ain't no weirder than your 35 year-old son that has been in college since 2001 and is still a freshman!"

Mayor Galley was now in a defensive stance as well, his fists balled up, his rounded belly jostling. "I told you Johnny is trying to find himself!"

"Hell, as long as that idiot's been lost, he could have found Neverland by now and the rest of his lost boy friends," Harlan spat at the Mayor.

Mayor Galley tried to do a fancy move with some Muhammad Ali footwork, but his belly was so large and his feet so small, that he only proceeded in tripping himself up and falling face first in the dirt. This brought all the women folk running as the DJ stopped playing the music. Chaos was two steps from taking over the awful scene. The whole thing was almost criminal as the fat man bent so far over, he looked like a caricature of the yard art of a fat lady bending over to scoop up eggs. By the time Orlando reached the fray, Jacquetta had taken a stand on top of the table. She clapped her hands three times.

It was an old classroom trick that she employed for a second time. The third time was the charm. All eyes were on her.

"Since we have everyone gathered around, my husband and I would like to make a special presentation. Orlando baby, get on up here," she said as he made his way through the small crowd.

Jacquetta called out, "Ms. Maggie Mae, we need you up here as well."

Maggie Mae made her way to the center of the crowd as people whispered and wanted to know what was happening. Orlando climbed up on the bench alongside his wife.

Orlando addressed the crowd, "As you all know, my father officially retired last year and handed the store over to me. Neither he nor my mother have ever had a chance to take a real vacation. So Mom... Dad, as a retirement gift to you, Jacquetta and I present you with a two month long vacation," he said as his mother's eyes began to tear up.

Harlan spoke, "Son, that is not necessary...you have a new wife...you will be starting a family soon...you don't need to..."

Orlando cut him off, "Dad, my wife came with enough stuff that the only thing we will need to buy in the next five years is groceries!" The crowd began to laugh. "If she keeps flirting with ole Jake over there, I know we will get the family discount on meats at the butcher shop!" This brought more laughter from the group.

Someone in the background yelled out, "Where are they going for two months?"

Mayor Galley mumbled loudly in the back, "I hope it's a trip to Hell you mean spirited old nail counting gas bag!"

Before Harlan could respond, Jacquetta spoke up. "Dad," she said with a wink. "You will fly from Valdosta to Seattle for four days in Washington State. We have rented you a car and mapped all of the places you two have wanted to see in this great country. Take your time as you drive back, as long as you are in Atlanta by September 15th, because you have a flight to New York for a three night stay. You will then fly from New York to Venice for a week-long stay. I booked you on the Eurail from Venice back in Switzerland where you will fly home. In between those times, you are free to sight see and rumble about, so get out that passport and you can get going!"

The crowd oohed and aahed as Harlan held Maggie Mae in his arms. "Venice, Maggie Mae....you always wanted to see Venice."

"Switzerland Harlan, can you believe it?" Maggie Mae said in disbelief.

Both Jacquetta and Orlando stepped down off the bench to be pulled into a hug by his parents. "You can't afford this for us son," Harlan whispered.

"We can. We have already done it. And you two deserve the time away. Enjoy yourselves," he told them as he handed them an envelope with their plane tickets.

The final surprise came from Orlando as Becca walked over to stand in the center of the group, trying to draw attention to her belly. A young couple walked over to join the melee of well-wishers to the Flynn's. They were really cute together. Orlando performed the introductions.

"Honey, this is Ethan and Janie Strom, they own The

Roxy bookstore. Remember I showed it to you on the way into Venture." He turned to the couple, "We'd love to have you guys over for dinner this week, if your schedule can work it out," Orlando said to Ethan.

Jacquetta smiled at Janie, who was a cute blond with a pixie hair cut that really suited her face. "Let me know what you would like me to bring," Janie said to her.

Becca was outdone. No one was paying any attention to her and by her standards that was completely unacceptable. "So what are we, chopped liver? You are in such a giving mood Orlando Flynn, I don't see you extending any benevolence towards us!"

Orlando didn't bat an eye. "You two can come too if you'd like, Jean Marc you are more than welcomed in our home," he said with a pause. Orlando turned to look at Becca's tummy. "But you have to take off that stupid fake belly."

Her mouth was wide open as she turned beet red all the way up her neck to the roots of her bottle blond hair. Orlando did not let up. "Becca, you aren't any more pregnant than I am. If you are, you aren't pregnant by him," he pointed to Jean Marc. "That man has spent more time watching my ass than yours!"

A buzz went through the crowd. People were gawking at Becca's stomach, and beginning the gossip that Orlando had feared. Right now, he was far more fearful of the look on his wife's face.

Harlan, always prepared to be the consummate host, stepped forward. "Okay folks, we have burgers, sausages and dogs on the grill. All this good food is ready to be eaten up and enjoyed. Come on, step right up," he shouted over the dull roar of the group. "Rodney, get some music going for the good people of Venture. Let's get this celebration moving."

Chapter 22 – Let There Be Fireworks

Jacquetta had very little to say through the fireworks display which occurred during the evening. The show was really nice but she was stuck on the rudeness of her husband to a woman who obviously had something serious going on in her head to fake a pregnancy. She could not wait to get into the truck to bring it up.

"It is obvious you are angry at me, so go ahead, and let me have it. However, whatever it is, we have to work it out before we go to bed, because I am not sleeping next to a pissed off woman," Orlando told her.

It was the inhale which made him pull over into an empty parking lot. She breathed deep before telling her husband, "I can't believe how you embarrassed Becca like that!"

"Becca embarrassed herself, showing up with that stupid mock pregnancy belly and a gay French dude," he said to Jacquetta.

"And speaking of that, how did you know he was gay?"

"You didn't recognize him? Jean Marc Beauvais, he's the son of the people who owned your favorite Pâtisserie in Paris. You know the one with the green hair and black fingernails!"

Her mouth made a wide O as she thought back to the angry kid who refused to go to the university. It still didn't change the subject in her mind. "Orlando, it doesn't change the fact that you were so rude to a woman you were engaged to and supposedly loved."

The details he wanted to tell her but hadn't had the

chance were all about to come out now. Either way, he was going to look like a manipulative asshole, but he did it all out of love. He only prayed she would understand.

"I didn't love her, I don't love her and I never proposed to that woman," he said coldly. He leaned back against the seat and waited for her scorn.

"Obviously, I missed something or I am not understanding, so you best start explaining right now Orlando Flynn," Jacquetta told him.

With ease and care he spoke of how a trip to the mall for Rebecca's birthday landed them in a jewelry store. Orlando explained how she tried on rings. "I turned around to say hi to an old friend, and she bought the ring," he told her.

"Even if you never proposed, you took advantage of all the benefits," she said in an accusatory tone.

His face in the dark cab of the truck was contorted. He flipped on the cabin light. Jacquetta jumped back at the anger she saw in his face. "What kind of man do you think I am? That is not who I am Jacquetta. To even suggest that I would do something so callous is offensive!"

"Are you telling me you didn't take advantage of an unstable woman?"

"That is exactly what I am telling you! I took advantage, but not as you think," he told her.

"Right now, you don't know what I am thinking about you," she mumbled under her breath.

Orlando dreaded this. He knew he should have said something sooner, and now he was boxed in. He explained that Saturday's in the store had been dedicated to workshop programs for women. The program provided free classes to women on laying tile, performing simple miter cuts and operating power tools. Orlando was still frowning. "The classes started out well, but those women...you guys say men are pigs, some of those women were worse. I have never heard so many innuendos with the word tool and screw. Becca showed up wearing the ring and all the crazy women hitting on me stopped. The only women who showed up to the classes from that point on were the ones who actually wanted to learn. So if you say that I took advantage, I did. This is a small town, I didn't want that type of reputation."

He was quiet as he turned to stare out the window. "My reputation means a lot to me," he told her.

"So are you saying that you and Becca never had sex," she asked.

"No. I didn't say that. Initially, when we started dating, we attempted a few times, but we just were not compatible. I no longer wanted to see her, and that's when she bought the ring," he told her.

"This is bullshit. It makes no sense at all. I don't understand what you are not telling me Orlando," she shouted at him.

"Jacquetta. I am a man. But I am not a man who lives by sex," he said. "The only woman that makes me go all bat shit crazy for sex is you!" The only way he could make her understand was to take her back to a time when he made the decision of what kind of man he wanted to be.

"Let me try to explain this the best way I can. When we were on missions, we were high on adrenalin; when the missions were done, it was a hard crash. Sometimes we were in towns and villages that weren't even on maps. Those people were eager to make money."

Orlando explained that for whatever proclivities a man had, the villagers and townspeople had an answer. "I need you to understand me 'Quetta. These people offered everything to a man that he could want for a minute of respite. Whatever got your junk hard, they had it. But that was not me. I had a reputation. I didn't judge the men if they needed to burn off some energy, but I retreated into my head."

A soft smile formed on his lips then disappeared. "I kid you not 'Quetta, if your thing was choking a bitch, these people would bring in six women for your bitch choking pleasure, but my men soon began to follow my example."

She sat, waiting for him to bring the ball all the way back to center court.

"In my head, I held onto the idea and image that when the mission was over, I was going to spend some time with you. I taught my men to focus on something they loved in the downtime that would keep them sane," he said.

"I need to know what your focus was on Orlando," she implored.

"I focused on the next time I would be with you."

Jacquetta was getting frustrated. "That makes even less sense, Orlando. Until a few days ago, you and I were never intimate," she said.

"In my head, we were," he said shyly. His cheeks were pink again. "In my head, I have made love to you on everything from a bed covered in rose petals to soft meadows filled with flowers. The fantasies I've had in my head about you kept me sane and it kept me alive. I have loved you for so long Jacquetta, sometimes I thought I would die if I couldn't get to you and be in your arms, even if you were only holding your friend."

The way he said it stole her breathe. This is what he was trying to tell her.

Orlando turned in the seat, his knees nearly hitting the steering wheel in the pick-up. "Did I do this all wrong, yes? Did I get lucky that it worked in my favor, yes? I have told you on so many occasions that I love you. I bought the damned house for you. I spent a year getting up my nerve to ask you to marry me as I worked on your wedding present. It took me a year, but I had to figure out how to get rid of Becca. She had booked a church for God's sake! So I started talking about Europe. I talked about it so much that she was itching to go. I sent her with the hopes that she would find something else to obsess over. When the two weeks turned into 3, and the three weeks turned into three months, I was pretty damned happy. By the time the six months came, the house was finished, and she called out of the blue saying she was coming back," Orlando told her.

None of this was sitting well with her at all. She even told him so in no uncertain words. She was vacillating between being flattered and being pissed off. She couldn't place her finger on why.

"I waited almost six years to make you my wife. I saved, I bought the perfect house, I put your studio in the backyard and I even fought through night terrors with you to call you my own. I don't understand your anger," he said.

"You lied to me," she told him.

"I did no such thing. I told you she was coming home pregnant with a French dude and I didn't want to be the laughing stock of the town. I called in the marker and you honored it. What did I lie about?"

He was right. He had not lied, but she still didn't like it. The feel of it was askew.

Orlando reached for her hands. "I cannot make love to a woman that I feel nothing for 'Quetta. When I connect my body to another person, I have to feel something powerful. Lawd knows I feels a mighty potent when I am with you. I have learned some of what pleases you and I am teaching you what pleases me. Our lovemaking is so good because I put in the work so I can know how to get you there. I want to make you happy. The more I learn, each time the train leaves the station, I plan for you to make at least three stops." He told her this part with a twinkle in his eye.

Her eyebrow arched slightly. "Stopping the train three times? Your metaphors are killing me."

"I am already up to two, and the train has only left the station three times," he said with a wink.

"It still makes no sense, Orlando. What is the point of all of this...?"

"The point, you daft, obstinate woman, is that I went through all of this to give you the life you wanted and deserved. A life full of love, with friends, family, and a house for all your collections and stuff," he said as he pulled her into his arms.

"And all of the knowing my body stuff..."

"Because, I want you to look at me the way my mother looks at my father. I want to be the man who makes you happy in life and in the bed. I want us to be so in tuned with each other that every time I lick my lips you will have to cross your legs. Each time you blow me a kiss I want my shit to get 16 year old hard. I want that kind of connection to my wife. I will never be insecure because I know the only man you are going to want is me! You already know the only woman I want is you."

"Lawd," she said as she cradled herself into his arms. "I don't even know what to say."

"Say that you love me. Say that everything I have done is worth it and our life together is going to be fantastic," he said as he kissed her temple.

Jacquetta squeezed his arm, speaking softly, "I love you Orlando, but I don't know about that part about our life being fantastic. We still have to find out why Becca went through so much trouble...six months in Europe, pretending to be pregnant, coming home with someone we would recognize..."

"I'm not sure what you mean," he said.

She sighed deeply. "I hope this is the end of her unstable behavior and not the beginning."

He laughed as he reached around her and cranked the truck, "We will find out this week over dinner."

Jacquetta wasn't too worried. Janie seemed like good people and at least she would have some backup. The comprehension that she needed backup was the thing that was worrying her the most. Becca had a look in her eyes that read trouble.

Chapter 23 - Undistinguished

Birds could be heard chirping from the oak trees in the backyard while Jacquetta sat quietly with her cup of coffee thinking, but not thinking. Hearing but not listening. Comprehending, yet not understanding.

Crazy.

In her mind, crazy was such a nasty word. It was one of those words people threw at others when someone else's actions doesn't match their expectations. She knew why it bothered her so much that everyone was quick to label Becca as crazy.

Life makes you crazy.

Jacquetta understood more than most that disappointment can shatter personal beliefs leaving the brain to create an alternate reality for coping with life's letdowns. At least that's what her therapist had told her. Jacquetta understood letdowns. Her life had far too many from people who claimed to love her or individuals who claimed to have her best interest at heart. From the moment she took a stand and did what was best for her own well-being, jerks who couldn't force her to behave as they thought was appropriate, labeled her as crazy.

I wasn't crazy.

Sebastian viewed her night terrors as crazy behavior. So crazy that he cared very little for helping her heal and move forward in her life with him. They could have been happy if he really wanted it. But he didn't. Truth was, he never really wanted her, but what she owned. It was part of the reason why she hadn't told her husband she had money.

Disappointment in Sebastian radiated through her, but in her head if she showed up to the church for the wedding maybe her groom to be would come as well. If he was actually serious about not marrying her, then she at least would be surrounded by family and friends who would offer her solace and support. Her second major disappointment came when she didn't receive either from family or friends. Well, except for Orlando who called every other week to make sure she was okay. He even surprised her one weekend by showing up and taking her on a quick trip to Nashville. Orlando was also the one who helped her decide about the family business.

When Jacquetta no longer wanted to own the furniture making business, she offered it to the family members who were employed by the company. Of course, none of them had any money to buy the operation, but they wanted her to man it so they could have jobs. The day she signed the paperwork selling it to a mid-sized furniture making company, everyone called her crazy.

Your grandparents are turning over in their graves.

I know your Mama is crying in Heaven over this honey chile.

How can you live with yourself? This business has been in the Mason family since they drew the Mason Dixon line.

"Do you have any money to buy it to help me keep it open and running?" she asked uncles, aunts and cousins.

"Well, naw...but...," was the answer she received from them all.

"But nothing! You have no idea what it takes to run this company or this business, so you cannot tell me what I need to do," she told them.

The same mumblings about her sanity was said when she packed up her grandparents' home and put everything in storage. There were too many memories in the house for her to stomach. A good number of the items she sold online, she even loaded up a rental car and hit the flea market one weekend to cull down the amount of items she had in storage.

Ever since that boy left her at the altar, she ain't been the same.

Lawd that chile dun lost her mind...

She's acting a little touched if you ask me...

But that was the problem, no one asked her. Jacquetta was pretty certain that no one asked Becca what she wanted either. It was easier to label her as crazy and dismiss her desire to have a normal life with a man like Orlando who would love her.

A wry smile crept into the corner of her mouth as she thought about her husband. A husband that knew she no longer had a whole family. Orlando was a man that knew how much a quaint garden meant with fresh herbs to cook special meals or pick tomatoes right from her backyard. Painting was her passion, but in her heart, she was a simple girl who wanted a simple life. A nice house with a painting studio in the backyard was what she told him she always wanted.

Orlando had given her everything she desired. All of it

was great, but she only wished she knew what he expected of her or what he wanted so that he could be happy. She had lived through one man's disappointment in her.

Jacquetta wasn't sure if she could survive another.

Chapter 24 – What a Week

Orlando slept until noon on that Sunday and Jacquetta did not bother him. After her morning coffee, she donned a smock and headed to her studio to paint. The painting of the small town with Flynn Hardware at the center was coming together nicely. Hopefully by the time her in-laws returned from their trip, it would be ready and the perfect gift for the retirees.

At the rate things were going that Sunday afternoon, she was unclear if her in-laws were ever going to make it out of the house. Several times she went over the maps and driving directions, but Maggie Mae seemed flummoxed by the whole concept. Finally, Jacquetta had enough. She grabbed her mother-in-law by the hands and leaned forward to whisper in her ear.

"For two months, Harlan is all yours. No hardware store, no nosey neighbors, no kids, no problems, just rest, relaxation and visiting places you always wanted to go," she told her mother-in-law.

Maggie Mae eyes misted up. Jacquetta looked at her closely. "Yes, this is the reward for being good parents and raising sons that you are proud of, good men — you have earned this."

"You are right, I have earned it dadgummit it!" Maggie Mae blurted out.

"Harlan!" She called to her husband. "We are getting the hell out here and going to have us some fun! I am even going to pack me some lingerie."

That part no one wanted to hear, especially Maggie Mae's sons, but it kicked off what could have possibly been one of the weirdest weeks of Jacquetta's life. The week was even odder than being kidnapped and used as the prize in a poker game. By the end of the week she finally understood why she was Orlando's wife and why she belonged in Venture, Georgia. Jacquetta also understood what her husband needed to be happy; her.

On Monday morning, Jacquetta tried to paint but no inspiration was coming to her, so she opted instead to bake. The first thing in the oven was a blueberry buckle. Since she had so many berries, she made blueberry turnovers as well. The smell must have wafted over to Ms. Marvin, who rang the doorbell to come and investigate.

Ms. Marvin was followed by Guy, and the old man across the street who loved to watch her butt as she worked in the yard. He took pride in telling her so as he ate a turnover. The turnovers she shared freely and even scored three recipes for the use of peaches.

A peach cobbler sounds really good for dessert on Friday.

Tuesday she received a call from the Dean at the college to come over in the afternoon for a tour. This really was not in her plans, but she donned a smart black suit, some mid-level heels, a pair of hose and headed over. The tour lasted all of 30 minutes and he sent her on her way with the understanding that she needed to get to HR before next week.

Dean Noitan said, "We have to get your badge, your access codes, and the class rosters for the day and night classes which will be mixed with grads and undergrads. Oh, before I forget, here is your text book." When she reached her car, her eyes were crossed, her body was sweaty and she really was kind of ticked off because she had not asked that man for a job. It had indeed been an odd Tuesday.

Jacquetta felt hopeful on Wednesday morning when she rose. She worked on the small town Americana painting, planted a tomato plant in the back yard, and sat on the deck enjoying the afternoon sun with a paperback. The moment she leaned back and rested her feet, she looked down the stairs to see Woodson standing there. He wanted nothing more than to see the house, have a cup of coffee and eat one of her blueberry turnovers that he'd heard so much about. He sat quietly with her on the back porch, looking at nothing in particular and enjoying his cup of Joe. The man had absolutely nothing to say to her with the exception of, "that is a good spot for that 'mater plant." After an hour, he stood, stretched, and said, "Nice visiting with you." With the same ease that he walked up to the back porch, was the same ease in which he left.

She mentioned his visit to Orlando after supper. "Hey, Woodson stopped by today," she told him.

Orlando answered drolly, "I bet that was an earth shattering conversation."

Jacquetta only smiled at him. "He enjoyed his visit."

"Glad to see you two getting along," Orlando answered in the same Devil-May-Care attitude. "Woodson doesn't like many people. He cares even less to spend time with women in a non-sexual way."

Her eyebrows shot up. "What in the hell does that mean?"

"It means he likes you as a person," Orlando said.

"Oh," was all she added. And that was how Wednesday ended.

Thursday brought a visit from Christopher. "I heard you will be teaching over at the University," he started as he came up to her on the porch.

"Yes, I will be teaching two art history classes," she told him.

"Mind if I get a cup of coffee?"

"Help yourself," she told him.

This day she was on the front porch potting some plants in the new green wood planters Orlando built for her. They were happily painted the same color green as the house. He said little as he sat on the porch, with a chunk of her blueberry buckle, staring out at the street.

"How do you talk to him?" Christopher asked.

Jacquetta looked up at her brother in law, "How do I talk to who?"

He bit into the buckle, his eyes rolled upwards. His mouth still full he said, "He says everything so flat, without emotion. The only time he has any emotion in his voice is when he is yelling at you."

She thought about it for a minute as she stood slowly. "When you work with soldiers, your orders have to be clear and succinct. There can be no room for interpretation, especially when mistakes can get you killed. He wants to make certain that what he is saying is not misunderstood."

"That makes sense," he said. He sat there as if the meaning of the universe had been revealed to him and he now understood his purpose in life. He watched her work for about an hour, saying nothing more as he waved at neighbors passing by. Like Woodson, he washed his cup, thanked her for the dessert and headed towards his fancy red car.

"You know Jacquetta," he said to her. "We never get to do this kind of stuff with our little brother. Sometimes, I feel as if I don't know him."

She put down the trowel and removed her gloves. She came to the end of the steps and looked him square in the face, "He is exactly who you think he is."

Christopher nodded his head and left. The only people left to make a visit was the two cousins. She would check with her husband to see if he wanted to have them over for dinner anytime soon.

Friday morning, she was preparing the house for the dinner guests and thought she would do something a little on the fancy side, and she pulled out a set of the good china. Since she had the good china, she grabbed the gold chargers, the fancy napkins and the bistro silverware. Her grandmother's hand-stitched table mats went under the chargers. The almost fancy lacy napkins were pressed, folded and placed in the center of the plates. Jacquetta went so far as to pull out the silver candle holders and the beeswax candles.

"A rib roast would be perfect for dinner with an endive salad and good bottle of red wine," she said aloud.

Instead of driving into town, she rode her bike to get a bit of exercise. *Why not?* She thought as she rode up to the front door of Flynn Hardware. She waved to Rodney and Jake Baldwin who was out front across the street at the butcher shop as she made her way to the back of the store to Orlando's office. He sat behind his desk, staring at the wall. The far-off gaze gave her a bit of a start, but suddenly he blinked, crossed himself and smiled.

Was he praying with his eyes open?

Jacquetta cleared her throat. Slowly his eyes came forward to look upon her form. He blinked several times, still saying nothing. He rubbed his eyes like he was tired and looked at her again.

She asked, "Orlando, are you okay?"

His eyes got wide. "Oh my goodness! You are actually standing there!" He said and started to laugh at himself.

"Were you imagining me...or something?" she asked.

He leaned back in the chair, "No... I...never mind, you will think I'm crazy."

There is that word again.

"No, I won't. Tell me what you were thinking," she said as she moved closer to the desk.

He pressed his lips together tightly before he exhaled a large gust of air. "I have imagined so many times you coming through that door to see me, simply to tell me that you love me and to get a kiss before you finished your errands. I have seen it in my head so many times...and to look up and actually see you standing there...I guess it threw me," he said sheepishly.

She moved closer to the desk and took a seat on his lap. He brushed a wayward strand of hair from her face and tucked it behind her ear.

"Is everything okay, or did you come to pick up some paints or something?" he asked her. His arms encircling her waist.

She leaned forward and planted a firm kiss on his lips. Smiling, she told him, "I stopped by to get a kiss, to tell you that I love you, and to make sure you're home in time to shower and change before our guests arrive." She kissed him again, this time, slipping in a little tongue.

"Enough of that, or my employees will come back here to find out why you are making funny noises," he told her as he lifted her from his lap. "Is there anything else you need Mrs. Flynn?"

"Yes, I need to hear some sexy words from my husband before I go over to the butcher shop to get a big hunk of meat from Jake," she told him with a flirty smile.

"You don't need a big hunk of meat from Jake. What you need is the handy tool I have over here to get any job you need completed," he said as he licked his lips. True to his word, feelings rushed through her straight into her pants and she squeezed her thighs together. Had she been seated, she would have involuntarily crossed her legs.

"That is not what I had in mind," she said with a furrowed brow.

Orlando pulled her into his arms. "So what you want to hear is how much I love you? You want me to plant sweet kisses on your neck and tell you how rich my world is now that you are in it full time. Is that what you need Mrs. Flynn?"

"Yes..." She answered huskily, swallowing hard as her body began to heat up. Her nipples hardened, her nectar was warming up, and she was two seconds from stripping down and mounting him on his desk.

He released her abruptly. "Well, you're not going to get it!" He broke into a gut busting laugh as he swatted her on the butt and pushed her out the door. "I'll be home early to lend a hand before the guests arrive," he said.

"You do that!" she said as she stepped outside of his office door. Her face was flushed as she left his office. "Damn," she said as she pressed her hands over her nipples to get them to flatten out. In her current state, she could probably poke someone's eye out.

One second sooner and she would have been able to see the pairs of ears who were tuning into the private conversation with her husband. A set of ears belonging to her father-in-law who was listening in from behind a crate full of bolts. He was supposed to be home packing to leave for Seattle next week. Rodney was listening in from behind a shelf of returned paints. The last set of ears belonged to none other than Becca Freeman whom had stopped in for a visit before she ran some errands to see if Orlando Flynn had ever really loved her.

All of the answers Becca needed would be provided to her in a mere couple of hours.

Chapter 25 – Dinner, Pie and Understanding

The rib roast was absolute perfection as she pulled it from the oven at 6:55 pm. The scalloped potatoes looked as if they had come from the pages of a magazine. The endive salads were plated as the doorbell rang exactly at 7:00 pm.

Orlando greeted the incoming guests. "Ethan, Janie, welcome. Come on in," he told them.

He showed them to the family room as he waited at the door for Becca and Jean Marc to get out of their car. At least tonight she wasn't wearing the ridiculous fake pregnancy belly. "Hey guys, come on in," he told them.

As expected, Jean Marc brought two bottles of wine, one for dinner and the other for dessert.

"Perfect!" Jacquetta told him as she took the wine from his hand. "Dinner is ready, if you would follow me to the dining room."

Janie was looking about the space, totally impressed with what she was seeing. "Oh my Gracious! I love these wall murals and furniture," she told her. "You have decorated the heck out of this house."

Jacquetta couldn't help but blush. "Thank you. I truly love this house. After dinner I will give you a tour."

Becca's lips were tight and Jacquetta picked up on it. "That also includes you Becca," she said with a genuine smile.

Janie asked, "How long have you guys had this house?"

"Orlando bought it a year ago as a wedding present for me, and he finished the repairs on it a few weeks before I moved down," Jacquetta said, keeping her eye on Becca.

"And the murals, who did you commission to paint those," Janie wanted to know.

"I painted them," Jacquetta said proudly.

Orlando returned with the open bottle of red wine that Jean Marc had brought along with the bottle of red that Jacquetta had picked up as well. "I have a feeling this is going to be a two bottle night."

The evening went far smoother than either of them had imagined. Janie and Jacquetta became immediate friends and Orlando and Ethan included Jean Marc in all the conversations.

"Ethan, how did you and Orlando meet, if you don't mind me asking?" Jacquetta wanted to know.

Ethan sipped at the wine. "Janie and I purchased an old music hall. Our bookstore is downstairs and we live upstairs. We were doing a lot of renovations, and to save money, some of the smaller jobs I did myself."

Janie cut her eyes at him. Ethan smiled. "Some of the jobs I had to do twice. The second time, I got some advice from my helpful hardware man over here."

Jean Marc's eyes kept wandering back to a painting on the dining room wall. "I have a painting very similar to this one but smaller in my patisserie in Paris," he said.

Jacquetta smiled. "The one in your shop is the first one in the Untitled Series. The one on the wall here is number 6. The one you have in your shop is the most valuable of the set."

The Frenchman was grinning at her. "I found that out.

Someone came into the shop and offered me $10,000 Euros for it."

"That is a tenth of its value!" Jacquetta told him. Everyone in the room looked at her.

Jean Marc asked, "Are you very familiar with this artist?"

"I am the artist," she said.

This raised every eyebrow at the table, including her husband. Jacquetta tried to play it off. "Yeah, no one gives a flip about my paintings in the US. In Europe, I sell extremely well," she said. "More wine anyone?"

Becca didn't like the idea of Orlando's wife being a great cook and a wonderful hostess. The house she hated from the day he bought it now looked fantastic. The wall murals were really cool and she had seen a great deal of Jacquetta's art when she was in Italy and France. It bugged her that Orlando's wife was also a famous painter.

As hard as she tried to swallow it all down, it was choking her. Becca blurted out, "So, let me get this straight. You are famous in Europe, you seem to be famous here in Venture, this dinner was fantastic, the house looks amazing and you have stolen my man! I think I hate you!"

Janie moved closer to Ethan, whispering under her breath, "I didn't know it was going to be dinner and a show. Pour me some more wine."

Jacquetta was cool about it all. "I have coffee on, can I get anyone a cup?"

"Oh you are going to ignore me...ignore the pain you are causing me...like I am someone who doesn't matter?" Becca said through choked tears.

"No Becca, I am going to ask you to come in the kitchen with me and help me get coffee while the men move to the den, with servings of this delicious cobbler," she told the woman as she doled out helpings of her peach cobbler.

Orlando jumped up from the table. "That is our cue, gents."

Once they entered the den. Ethan spoke briefly about the space and talked about having a man cave in their next place. Orlando shared some ideas with him on the subject before turning his attention to Jean Marc. "So, how are you enjoying your visit to Venture, Georgia?"

Jean Marc sighed deeply, "I must leave soon. Becca's mother consistently makes French fries every night thinking she is cooking me French food."

"Whaaaaa?" Ethan said as he fell back into the couch falling over in a fit of laughter. Jean Marc did not find the humor. "Last night, I took over the kitchen and cooked us a meal. I was uncertain if I was going to die first of clogged arteries or clogged bowels!"

This lightened the mood for the men who enjoyed the sweetness of Jacquetta's cobbler. In the kitchen, Janie followed along behind the two ladies, standing far enough away in case anything came to blows. Jacquetta poured the coffee into cups as each lady carried one to the den for the men, walking calmly back to the kitchen. Becca said nothing as Jacquetta began to tidy up. Janie lent a hand and Becca followed suit.

The thick air seemed to thin out as the women focused

on the tasks of putting away the leftovers and making to-go plates. This is when Jacquetta addressed Becca, her voice soft and non-accusatory, "I'm not sure of your train of thought on the whole fake pregnancy thing...how did you think it was going to work?"

Red faced, embarrassed, but feeling a need to confess, Becca spoke. "I was going to tell Orlando that I lost the baby. We would have gotten back together and I would have given him the sons that he wanted," she said softly.

"And the whole fake engagement...?" Jacquetta asked.

"He went along with it, so I thought he wanted to be married to me as well. I knew in my heart there was someone else. Even when he touched me, his mind was elsewhere, he only made love to me once, and it felt like he did it out of pity. I don't even think he enjoyed it enough to finish." Becca confessed. "I knew he loved someone else...I figured if, I stepped out of the picture for just a minute, that everything would fall into place for us...that he would miss me and want me back..."

Jacquetta surprised both women by walking over to Becca and giving her a hug. "There is a man out there waiting to love you. Never, ever should you compromise yourself to fit the model of what you think a man wants. If he doesn't see the value you add to his life, then he is not worth your time."

Janie's eyes were wide. "Jacquetta, where were you when I had a nutty bitch try to kill Janie?"

"What?" Both Becca and Jacquetta asked at the same time.

"Yeah, she set Janie's building on fire with Janie still in it," Janie said with her mouth twisted.

Becca asked the question Jacquetta was thinking, "Why do you keep referring to yourself in third person?"

Janie picked up her glass of wine. "I have to when some shit is so unbelievable that the regular me can't even process it. This is like a whole out of body experience. You, the fake pregnancy belly, the gay French boy toy...Janie can't believe any of that stuff either!"

It was the look on Becca's face that made them stop and stare at her. "You know the Europeans are more open than we are. He isn't totally gay. That man have me seeing stars when he makes love to me!"

All three women burst into laughter.

In the other room, all three men relaxed a bit more. Jean Marc looked at Orlando. "You are a very lucky man."

"You have no idea," Orlando told him. "Gentlemen raise your cups, a toast to...hell whatever makes you happy!" Jacquetta made him happy.

He was happier than he had ever been in his life.

Chapter 26 – Making a Life

"Orlando," she whispered into his ear. "Wake up Sweetie, you are going to be late for work."

He rolled over in the bed, throwing a hairy leg on top of hers. "I took the weekend off. Woodson is in charge of the store, I promoted Rodney to evening manager, and most weekends will be reserved for my wife."

She planted a kiss loaded with morning breath on his cheek. "I feel so special."

"Because you are, my lovely lady," he told her as he pulled her into his arms. "I don't know what you said to Becca, but she seemed a whole lot better when she left."

Her fingers slipped under his shirt, massaging his belly. "All she wanted was to be loved. I think it's all anyone wants Orlando, she just chose a man who loved someone else."

He said nothing for a while as his fingers caressed the bare skin of her shoulders. "I fell in love with you the second time I paid you a visit in Naples. I had been on a shitty mission...I saw things done to children and young boys that really messed with my head. When I called you and told you I was coming, you heard something in my voice."

"Was that the weekend I got the NATO pilots to fly us to Greece?"

"Yes, and we spent the day on the beach, drank Ouzo, sang songs and you taught me my infamous dance moves," he laughed. "I never spent a better weekend in my life that did not involve sex. From that day forward, I could not wait to see you. To talk to you, to hear you laugh...I love to be around you."

She cuddled closer to him. "What if I had married Sebastian?"

"I knew that was not going to work out for you," he said confidently.

"I am not sure how you knew that," she said lightly.

At the risk of sounding arrogant, he spoke from his heart, "The same way I knew the only woman for me was you."

"Still not clear on your reasoning," she said as her hand slid lower.

"I knew Jacquetta Flynn, that wimpy Sebastian wasn't man enough for you because I set the standard of the man you wanted as a mate. I wasn't afraid of your night terrors, I held and calmed you on nights that you didn't even ask me to, and if I might add, since the first time I made love to you, there has not been another attack."

She sat up in the bed. "Aren't you full of yourself?"

"No baby, you no longer have the terrors because you feel safe," he said to her. He used his hand to push her back on the bed, she lay on her back looking up at him, her heart nearly bursting with love for the man. Orlando's fingers tugged at the top of her pajama pants, his fingers slipping inside the pajama shorts, then into her undies. His eyes never left hers as his fingers moved, opening his wife to the first stage of her pleasure.

He knew it was a long way from her being healed, but this was as close as they could come at this point. Orlando made love to her slowly, whispering encouraging words in her ear as his body became an instrument of her pleasure. He knew she was rounding the crest for her first stop on the pleasure train, he picked up his pace enough to get her there, "On me, 'Quetta," he commanded as she bucked her hips against him, crying out his name. That was only her first one, he had learned what it took to get her there and he wasn't going to disappoint the lady. He took his time with his wife, ensuring two more stops before he brought the train into the station. Sweat soaked, they clung to each other in the early morning light.

His thumb rubbed her hip as something which had been in the back of his mind occurred to him at the dumbest possible moment. "Wait a minute. You sold your grandparents house, you sold the furniture business and you are famous in Europe. Jacquetta, are we rich?"

She pulled away from him and started for the kitchen to make coffee, wearing only her slippers. "No, I'm rich. You own a hardware store in Yahoo, Georgia!"

Orlando moved like a flash out of the bed as she ran down the hall toward the kitchen. "I thought we agreed that what is mine is yours and what is your is mine?" He chased her around the island until she finally collapsed on the couch.

"I didn't agree to no such thing Orlando Flynn!" She giggled. Orlando stood over her, reaching downwards just as his cell phone rang. He recognized Guy's number.

"This is Flynn," he answered into the phone.

A raspy voice came over the line, "Move your naked

candy ass three steps to the left so I can get an eyeful of my "Quetta!"

He hung up the phone. "Guy said good morning." Orlando's head snapped around as he ran to the window and closed the blinds. "Today we are going shopping for some damned drapes!"

"I understand why you always keep the phone so close by you. It's for Guy right? In case he is in trouble and calls..."

He put down the phone as he scooped his wife into his arms, "Yeah. I will be so glad when that dirty diaper moves. Let's get a hot shower and get this Saturday going. What do you want to do today?"

"Whatever you want Mr. Flynn," she told him.

For Orlando, he wanted to board the train once more in the shower and make a couple of quick stops in happy land. Jacquetta seemed okay with it as well.

Epilogue

It was a very cool Christmas morning when Jacquetta slumped her way to the kitchen for a cup of hot tea. Six months of marriage really agreed with her as she started each morning with a smile. The lonely life she led before devoid of any real friends had been replaced by Friday night dinners with different friends hosting the couples in their homes.

The first Friday of the month belonged to she and Orlando. The second Friday was hosted by Ethan and Janie, who had easily become her best friend. Courtney, the bank manager and his wife Rochelle took over the third Saturday. New neighbors moved into Guy's house about four months ago after Marla moved her dad to Valdosta. The house sold quickly to Jack and Samantha Fischer, who also became fast friends and took over the fourth Friday. They were vegans which always made Orlando eat vast quantities of meat before they went over for dinner.

The family which no longer desired to speak to her was replaced by a new family of crazy, red-necks who loved to tell everyone, they had a cousin married to a black woman. Thanksgiving was an interesting spectacle as things that lived in the woods were marinated overnight in milk and served at the annual Thursday evening feast. Coon, possum and squirrel were not the things she liked to eat, nor anything she ever wanted to sample. It didn't matter to her what was on the table because oddly enough, she felt welcomed and loved.

This morning she was ready to present to her husband a gift that she had been working on for several months. He made his way down the hall, wearing jammies, which he wore more often than being au natural, since Samantha had caught a glimpse of his nude act.

"Merry Christmas 'Quetta," he said as he wrapped his arms around her waist planting a light kiss on her neck.

"Merry Christmas Mr. Flynn. I want you to open your present," she told him as she pulled him into the living room and grabbed a package from under the tree.

"You sure you don't want to wait until after breakfast, some steak and eggs sound really good," he told her.

"You are such a carnivore."

"There are some things that men like to eat on a regular basis - a good steak is also on my list," he winked at her.

Jacquetta rolled her eyes. "Come on open your present."

Orlando knew it was a painting, but he was uncertain of what. The house was loaded with her art and small paintings of everything in Venture, including The Roxy, Janie and Ethan's book store. He was almost disappointed that she hadn't gotten him a new set of golf clubs. The ones he had were a hand-me-down set from his dad.

A faint smile was given as he pulled back the brown wrapper. The image before him stole his breath. The painting was made from a portrait of him and Jacquetta in Versailles. He remembered the picture but in her arms instead of the stray puppy they had saved from the overflowing water in the streets, there was a small child. Orlando stared at the painting, uncertain why the child had no face.

"It's not finished," he said softly.

"No, not yet," she responded.

"Why doesn't the child have a face?"

She touched his hand. "Because I don't know the sex of our baby."

His eyes came up slowly as he looked at her stomach. "Seriously 'Quetta? We are having a baby?"

"Well, in seven months, I am only two months along," she told him.

He sat there staring absently like he had been doing the day she walked into his office in the hardware store. He blinked furiously and then slowly closed his eyes. They stayed closed for several minutes as he crossed himself. A tear escaped the corner of his eye that he wiped away with his thumb.

"Orlando, are you okay or did you dream about this moment as well?"

"I have dreamed about this moment all of my life. To have you deliver the news, well, I am...I ...thank you. I am so happy. This is the best Christmas present ever..."

The phone rang as he reached for his wife to pull her into an embrace. He was torn between answering it and holding the mother of his soon to be child.

"Merry Christmas this is Flynn," he said into the line. His eyes were still on his wife as his fingers caressed her cheek.

A raspy voice came through the line, "Merry Christmas you candy ass weirdo! Have you knocked up my 'Quetta yet or do I need to come up there and show you how a real man handles a beautiful woman like that beauty you got lucky enough to marry. I bet you tricked her into it, you knocked kneed knob gobbler!"

Orlando hung up the phone without replying. "That was Guy, he said Merry Christmas."

"I am so in love with you Orlando Flynn, I am sometimes scared that I will wake up and none of this is real," she told his as she sat in his lap.

"It's real Mrs. Flynn and so is our love," he told her.

The presents under the tree for her, she cared very little about. The one thing she really wanted she now had. A whole family again.

-Fin —

Thank you for reading this latest installment in the town of Venture, Georgia where I first introduced readers to Janie & Ethan. I hope you have read about the town of Venture, because we will journey back there several times as I introduce you to new and fun characters.

Come on in and start <u>Turning the Page</u>.

About the Author

About the Author

Olivia Gaines is the award winning author of Thursday's in Savannah and numerous bestselling novellas and books, including *Two Nights in Vegas, A Few More Nights,* and has had several number one best sellers with *The Blakemore Files* including *Being Mrs. Blakemore* and *Shopping with Mrs. Blakemore.*

She lives in a small town in Georgia, with her husband, son and snotty cat, Katness Evermean.

Connect with Olivia on her Facebook page at https://www.facebook.com/Ogaines or her website at http://ogaines.com.

Olivia Gaines

An Untitled Love

Made in the USA
Columbia, SC
18 March 2020

89473373R00107